HAMID ISMAILOV

TRANSLATED FROM THE RUSSIAN
BY ANDREW BROMFIELD

Вундеркинд
Ержан

GIFT

AUTHOR

Born in 1954 in Kyrgyzstan, Hamid Ismailov moved to Uzbekistan as a young man. He writes in both Russian and Uzbek, and his novels and poetry have been translated into many European languages, including German, French and Spanish. In 1994 he was forced to flee to the UK because of his 'unacceptable democratic tendencies'. He now works for the BBC World Service. His first novel to be published in English, *The Railway*, appeared in 2006, followed by *A Poet and Bin-Laden* in 2012. His work is still banned in Uzbekistan today.

TRANSLATOR

Andrew Bromfield's career of more than twenty years as a translator of Russian literature had its beginnings in Moscow during the perestroika period. In 1991 he was a founding editor of the journal *Glas: New Russian Writing*. He has translated works by Boris Akunin, Vladimir Voinovich and Irina Denezhkina, among other writers.

MEIKE ZIERVOGEL
PEIRENE PRESS

Like a Grimms' fairy tale, this story transforms an innermost fear into an outward reality. We witness a prepubescent boy's secret terror of not growing up into a man. We wander in a beautiful, fierce landscape like no other in Western literature. And by the end of Yerzhan's tale we are awestruck by our human resilience in the face of catastrophic, man-made, follies.

First published in Great Britain in 2014 by
Peirene Press Ltd
17 Cheverton Road
London N19 3BB
www.peirenepress.com

First published under the original Russian language title
Вундеркинд Ержан by Druzhba Narodov, 2011

ISBN 978-1-908670-14-4

Designed by Sacha Davison Lunt
Photographic image: Red Edge/Juliette Mills
Typeset by Tetragon, London
Printed and bound by T J International, Padstow, Cornwall

This translation was effected under the auspices of
the Mikhail Prokhorov Foundation TRANSCRIPT to
Support Translations of Russian Literature.

Supporting
the translation
of Russian
literature

transcript

Peirene

HAMID ISMAILOV

TRANSLATED FROM THE RUSSIAN
BY ANDREW BROMFIELD

The
Dead Lake

Between 1949 and 1989 at the Semipalatinsk Nuclear Test Site (SNTS) a total of 468 nuclear explosions were carried out, comprising 125 atmospheric and 343 underground blasts. The aggregate yield of the nuclear devices tested in the atmosphere and underground at the SNTS (in a populated region) exceeded by a factor of 2,500 the power of the bomb dropped on Hiroshima by the Americans in 1945.

This story began in the most prosaic fashion possible. I was travelling across the boundless steppes of Kazakhstan on a train. The journey had already taken four nights. Trackmen at remote way stations tapped on the wheels with their hammers, swearing in Kazakh. I felt myself swell with a secret pride that I could understand them. During the day the platforms and corridors of the carriages were awash with women's and children's versions of the same tongue. At every way station the train was boarded by ever more vendors – all women – peddling camel wool, sun-dried fish or simply pellets of dried sour milk.

Of course, that was a long time ago. Perhaps nowadays things have changed. Although somehow I doubt it.

Anyway, I was standing at one end of the carriage, gazing out – for the fourth day already – at the dreary, monotonous steppe, when a ten- or twelve-year-old boy appeared at the other end. He held a violin and suddenly started playing with such incredible dexterity and panache that at once all the compartment doors slid open and passengers' drowsy faces appeared. What they heard wasn't some flamboyant Gypsy refrain, or even a distinctive local melody; no, the boy played Brahms, one of the famous *Hungarian Dances*. He played as he walked, coming towards me. Then, just as he had the entire carriage gaping after him open-mouthed, he broke off in mid-note. He slung the violin back over his shoulder like a rifle. 'Wholesome local beverage – entirely organic!' he exclaimed in a thick, adult voice. He swung a canvas sack down off his other shoulder and pulled out an immense plastic bottle of a yoghurt drink, either *ayran* or *kumis*. I approached him, without even knowing why.

'Young lad,' I said, 'how much is your *kumis*?'

'In the first place, it's not my *kumis* but the mare's, and in the second place, it's not *kumis* but *ayran*, and finally, I'm not a young lad!' the urchin replied defiantly in perfect Russian.

'You're not a little girl though, are you?' I clumsily attempted to smooth things over.

'I'm not a woman, I'm a man! Like to try me? Drop your breeches!' the youngster snarled back, loud enough for the whole carriage to hear.

I didn't know whether to be angry or to try to soothe him. But after all, this was his land and I was the visitor here, so I softened my own tone of voice to ask, 'Have I insulted you in some way? If I have, I'm sorry... But you play Brahms like a god...'

'There's no point insulting me. I'll do any insulting there is to be done... I'm no young lad. Never mind my size, I'm twenty-seven. Got that?' he asked in a voice lowered to a half-whisper.

Now that staggered me.

So that's the beginning of the story. As I've already said, he looked like a perfectly normal ten- or twelve-year-old boy. No anomalous features marked him out as a midget or a dwarf, no disproportionate limbs, no wrinkles on the face or anything of the kind.

Naturally, I didn't believe him at first, and it was obvious from my expression.

'Right, here, take a look at my passport,' he said, tugging the document out of his inside pocket with a well-practised movement.

While he sold his *ayran* to women who fussed over him delightedly ('Where did you learn to play like that?' 'Can you play "Dark Eyes"? How about "Katyusha"?'), I stood there like a fool, my eyes wandering between the official document and his face. Everything matched. Looking out at me from the photo was the unspoilt face of a child.

'What's your name?' I asked.

'Yerzhan,' he replied curtly, jabbing his finger at the passport.

'Can I buy... some of your... I mean some *ayran*?' I gabbled in a rather ludicrous, apologetic tone.

Taking back his passport, he replied, 'Brahms, you say? The last bottle, take it. I've sold the lot...'

We went into my compartment to fetch the money, and since the old man in the place opposite mine was sound asleep, I asked Yerzhan to take a seat, adding that it made no sense to stand when we could sit…

'Does anything make any sense?' he retorted, suddenly prickly again, and his question seemed to be addressed, not to me, but to this train galloping across the steppe, to this blazing steppe spread out across the earth, to this earth, adrift between light and darkness, to this darkness, which…

Part One

Do
Before

Yerzhan was born at the Kara-Shagan way station of the East Kazakhstan Railway, into the family of his grandfather, Daulet, a trackman, one of those who tap wheels and brake shoes at night and during the day, following a phone call from a dispatcher, go out to switch the points so that some weary old freight train can wait while an express or passenger special like ours hurtles straight through the junction.

The column for 'Father' in his birth certificate had remained blank, except for a thick stroke of the pen, and the only entry, under 'Mother', was for Kanyshat, Daulet's daughter, who also lived at the way station (which everyone called a 'spot'). The 'spot' consisted of two railway houses. In one lived, in addition to Yerzhan, his grandfather and mother, his grandmother, Ulbarsyn, and her younger son, Yerzhan's uncle, Kepek. The second way-station house was occupied by the family of Grandad Daulet's late shift partner, Nurpeis: his widow, Granny Sholpan, her son, Shaken, with his city bride, Baichichek, and their daughter, Aisulu. Aisulu was a year younger than Yerzhan. Nurpeis himself had fallen under a non-scheduled train.

And that was the entire population of Kara-Shagan, if you didn't count the fifty or so sheep, three donkeys, two camels and the horse, Aigyr, all owned between the two families. There was also the dog, Kapty. But he lived with Aisulu most of the time, so Yerzhan didn't think of him as his own. Just as he didn't take into account the clutch of dusty chickens with a pair of loud-voiced cocks, since they multiplied and decreased in numbers in such a mysterious fashion that none of the Kara-Shaganites ever knew how many of them there were.

Multiplying in a mysterious fashion is a relevant point here, since in fact no one, except perhaps God, knew how Yerzhan's mother, Kanyshat, became pregnant with him and by whom. Cursed by her father from that time on, she never spoke a word about it to her 'immaculately conceived' son. And all that Yerzhan knew – from what Granny Ulbarsyn told him – was that at the age of sixteen Kanyshat had run into the steppe after her silk scarf, which had blown off. The steppe wind lured her on, further and deeper, as if teasing her, on and on towards the sunset. And what happened after that was so fantastic that Yerzhan couldn't make any sense of it. The sun was already sinking when suddenly it soared back up into the sky, glowing brightly. A tremor ran through the earth from the horizon. A whistling wind sprang up out of nowhere, then faded away for an instant, only to reverse its direction with a mighty rush so sudden that the dust of the steppe swirled up to the heavens in a black, hurtling tornado. And when Kanyshat, more dead than alive, discovered that she was at the bottom of a gully, there standing over her scratched and bloody body was a creature who looked like an alien from another planet, wearing a spacesuit.

Three months later, when she began to show, Daulet, foaming with rage, brutally beat and cursed her for ever. If Kepek and Shaken hadn't pulled the old man away from his half-dead daughter and dragged him to Granny Sholpan's house, neither Kanyshat nor her son would have been long for this world.

Since that day Kanyshat hadn't spoken a word.

Although Yerzhan's mother was silent, the other women, and especially the two grannies, Ulbarsyn and Sholpan, loved to tittle-tattle, as Grandad Daulet called it.

Yerzhan recalled vicious winter nights. Whistling, windswept snow forced its way in through every crack in the window.

'There in the ninth heaven grows Tengri's sacred tree, *Kayin*, and hanging on its branches, like a little leaf, is the *kut*.'

Yerzhan had climbed into bed with Granny Ulbarsyn under her camel-wool blanket. She scratched his anus, which itched with little squirming worms.

'What's a *kut*?' asked Yerzhan, still shivering from the cold. He was surprised by the similarity of this word to the word for 'backside' – *kyot*.

'It's happiness. It's when you're warm and well fed,' Granny answered, and carried on with her story.

'When you were going to be born, your *kut* fell off that tree into our house, down through the chimney. Everything follows the will of Tengri and our mother Umai. The *kut* fell into your mother's tummy and in her womb it took the form of a little red worm…'

'Is it him you're scratching out of my backside?'

Granny tittered and slapped Yerzhan on his little cheek with the same wrinkled hand that had just scratched his backside.

'You little chatterbox, sleep, or Mother-Umai will get angry and take away your *kut*!'

On another night the boy stayed at Granny Sholpan's house because he wanted to be near little Aisulu, whose ear he had already nibbled so that he would marry her later. And this time Granny Sholpan told him her version of his conception and birth and wove a story about Tengri's son, Gesar, into it.

'Tengri sent Gesar to the earth, to a kingdom in the steppe where there was no ruler.'

'You mean to us?' Yerzhan immediately butted in. But Granny Sholpan's fearsome glance cut him short.

'So that no one would recognize him' – the old woman pinched Yerzhan's nose – 'Gesar came down to earth as a frightful, snotty-nosed little scamp like you!'

Yerzhan started whining. His nose was hurting. And since Granny Sholpan didn't want to wake up Aisulu, who was asleep in her cot next to them, she let go of his nose before she continued.

'Only his uncle, Kara-Choton – the same kind of uncle

as Kepek is to you – learnt that Gesar wasn't just an ordi-
nary little boy, but heaven-born, and he started to bully
his nephew in order to destroy him before he grew up. But
Tengri always saved Gesar from Kara-Choton's wicked
tricks. When Gesar turned twelve, Tengri sent him the
fleetest steed on earth, and Gesar won the famous horse
race to marry the beautiful Urmai-sulu and conquered
the throne of the steppe kingdom.'

'Kazakhst—' Yerzhan started to say, but stopped short
when he spotted the sharp glint in Granny Sholpan's
eyes again.

She went on: 'The bold Gesar did not enjoy his happiness
and peace for long. A terrible demon, the cannibal Lubsan,
attacked his country from the north. But Lubsan's wife,
Tumen Djergalan, fell in love with Gesar and revealed her
husband's secret to him. Gesar used the secret and killed
Lubsan. Tumen Djergalan didn't waste any time and gave
Gesar a draught of forgetfulness to drink in order to bind
him to her for ever. Gesar drank the draught, forgot about
his beloved Urmai-sulu and stayed with Tumen Djergalan.

'Meanwhile, in the steppe kingdom, a rebellion arose
and Kara-Choton forced Urmai-sulu to marry him. But
Tengri did not desert Gesar and freed him of the enchantment on the very shore of the Dead Lake, where Gesar
saw the reflection of his own magical steed. He returned
on this steed home to the steppe kingdom and killed
Kara-Choton, freeing his Urmai-sulu…'

By now Yerzhan had warmed up nicely in Granny
Sholpan's cosy bosom and was fast asleep. In his dream,

though, he continued the adventure and rode the steed and freed Urmai-sulu.

Steppe roads, even if they are railroads, are long and monotonous, and the only way you can shorten the journey is with conversation. The way Yerzhan told me about his life was like this road of ours, without any discernible bends or backtracking. His story ran on and on, just as the wires outside the window ran from post to post, accompanied by the beat of the wheels' hammering. He recalled his distant childhood running back and forth between his house and Aisulu's house. Not only to look at the still-speechless beauty, whose ear he had nibbled in token of an early engagement, but mostly for the sake of his uncle Shaken's glittering metal objects. Shaken used to disappear on his work shifts for months at a time. He worked somewhere in the steppe. But more about that later. Just as we shall talk later about Shaken's television, which he brought back from the city.

But before that… Before that:

'All women ever want to do is wag their tongues!' Grandad Daulet said, and tied the young tot on his back with his belt and climbed up on to his piebald grey horse. It was a spring day. Grandad left the railway line in the care of his son, Kepek, and they rode out into the steppe. They galloped in silence over the damp grass and tulips, galloping, so it seemed, for no reason at all. And the wind, still chilly round the edges, scorched Yerzhan's cracking cheeks.

They galloped as far as a gully with sparse hills scattered beyond it.

'This is where we found you...' the old man said.

And there beyond the gully with the noisy spring river at its bottom, on the far side of the wooden suspension bridge, barbed wire extended right across the steppe. Grandad reined in his exhausted steed and waved towards the fence with his whip. 'The Zone!' he exclaimed. And at that moment a fly started buzzing in the boy's ear, a gadfly, the kind that circled above their cows on lazy days – a gadfly that became the droning word: Zone...

And the word began buzzing around in the child's imagination.

Uncle Shaken worked as a watchman in the Zone.

The old man untied Yerzhan from his back and laid out the belt for both of them to sit on. He unslung his *dombra* from his shoulder and filled the ravine with the sound of his song:

> *When I am one, I'm in the cradle,*
> *When I am five, I am God's own creature,*
> *When I am six, I'm like the birch pollen,*
> *When I am seven, I'm the earth's dust and its rot,*
> *When I am ten, I'm like a suckling lamb,*
> *And at fifteen I frolic like an elf and gnome...*

How could Yerzhan have guessed then that this ancient song – God knows how it had come to Grandad Daulet's soul – was about him, about his future life?

Gesar's story had sunk deep into Yerzhan's heart. And as Granny Ulbarsyn picked out from the boy's hair the lice which had grown fat over winter, Yerzhan asked her about Gesar's special features and how he could be recognized.

'When Gesar was a frightful, snot-nosed little urchin, he didn't have a willy,' she replied, and hoped to have stopped her squirming grandson from pestering her further. She needed him to keep still for an hour or so to deal with the lice, and nits too, and then wash his head with sour milk.

Once that was done, she asked him to take off his underpants. She searched for the nits between the seams and clicked them to death between her fingernails. But Yerzhan could no longer wait. He ran off bare-bottomed to Aisulu behind her house. There they took turns to contemplate his tiny, wrinkly willy and compared it to snot-nosed little Aisulu's enviable lack of any such item.

The boy also kept a close eye on his lazy uncle, Kepek, just in case he might try to bully his nephew. Kepek, however, spent most of his days sprawled on the only bedstead in the house, while at night-time he took his ageing father's place at the points or walked round the night trains with the family hammer.

Sometimes Kepek came home in the early morning rip-roaring drunk and turned the whole house upside down without any rhyme or reason, swearing and cursing. Granny Ulbarsyn's gasping and sighing woke Yerzhan up. And he was prepared for a sly beating from his own flesh and blood. But his uncle just shouted that he was going to leave this place for ever, that he was sick and tired of everything here, fuck this rotten life to hell! And then he leapt up onto his father's grey horse and galloped off into the vast steppe just as the darkness was dispersing. And Kepek's voice and his presence and his anger dispersed with it.

Granny Ulbarsyn's story wasn't the only thing that had sunk deep into Yerzhan's heart. Grandad's *dombra*-playing stayed with him too. When no one was looking the boy took the instrument down from its nail high up on the wall. And while his grandfather tapped with the hammer on railway carriages, Yerzhan strummed the *dombra* secretly, imitating the old man's knitted brows and hoarse voice. It didn't take long before he picked out a few familiar melodies and then, with the keen eye he used to keep watch on Uncle Kepek's behaviour, he followed and memorized his grandad's finger movements. And the next day, when Daulet wasn't there and Granny Ulbarsyn was visiting Granny Sholpan's house, the boy zealously repeated the same run of the fingers. Very quickly and inconspicuously he learnt almost all Grandad's repertoire.

But it wasn't Grandad who caught him at it, and not even Granny Ulbarsyn. It was Kepek, who wandered into the wrong room yet again in a drunken state. How fervently he kissed every one of his little nephew's fingers, how he slavered over them with his drunken spittle. 'Ah, sublime dark power! Ah, sublime dark sound!' he exclaimed, swaying his shaggy head wildly. That evening a slightly more sober Kepek gathered both families in front of the house and called his three-year-old nephew out of the door. The uncle announced that a concert was about to commence. And Yerzhan gave his first ever public performance, sitting in the doorway of his house.

His grandad was so moved that he retuned the *dombra* on the spot, changing from right tuning to left, from lower to higher, so that the boy could more easily sing along. He also now tutored his grandson every evening, recalling old melodies and ancient songs forgotten since the days of his youth. Within three months Yerzhan mastered everything that his grandad had accumulated in his entire lifetime – both melodies and verses. The little boy imbibed the centuries-old wisdom of the Kazakh, preserved in song, just as the steppe earth soaks up the rains of spring, transforming it into green tamarisk and feather grass, into scarlet poppies and tulips.

The high-soaring mountain is well suited
To the shadow running from it.

The deep-flowing river is well matched
To its meadowsweet-smothered bank.
The stout-hearted djigit *is well suited*
To the spear raised up in his hand.
The prosperous djigit *is well matched*
To the good he does for others.
The white-bearded elder is well suited
To the blessing of his retinue.
The affluent woman is well matched
To her plump goatskin of kumis.
The fresh young bride is well suited
To her little suckling babe.
When a maiden reaches the age of fifteen years,
More rumours are woven around her than braids
in her hair.
The only one guilty of all this falsehood
Is the black sheep among her kin.

'We shall not merely catch up with the Americans, but overtake them!' Shaken called out when he heard four-year-old Yerzhan sing this song. And the next time he returned from his shift, he didn't bring back a glittering metal object but a new type of *dombra*. Only a thousand times shinier. He called it a 'violin'.

This violin didn't have three strings, but four. At first Yerzhan tired to play it like a *dombra*. A muted and thin sound emerged. Shaken reached into his briefcase and pulled out a stick that looked like a whip. He called it a 'bow'. 'I'll show you!' he said, and began rubbing the stick against the strings. But now they emitted no sound whatsoever. 'Everything needs grease!' Grandad Daulet laughed out loud and fetched some wax and coated the instrument and its bow. As the bow touched the strings the instrument began to squeak. 'Give! Give!' Yerzhan pulled the violin from his grandfather's hands. That day he corroded everyone's ears. Only drunken Uncle Kepek was so touched that he burst into tears and said, 'I know a Bulgarian violinist! Pedo is his name. And true, he might be a paedo! But tomorrow we'll go to him!' In actual fact the Bulgarian violinist was called Petko, but Uncle Kepek didn't know how to pronounce his name properly.

The next day Kepek seated his nephew on a camel and the two of them set off across the railway line into the steppe. They rode for a long time until they reached a place with cabin trailers, excavators and all sorts of heavy equipment. There was no railway nearby, and metal lay about in heaps. They dismounted from their camel, tethered it to a solitary tamarisk bush and went into one of the trailers. Inside the air was smoky. Men sat around playing a noisy game. Yerzhan started to cough and Kepek told Petko they'd wait outside for him. Petko was a short man with shifty eyes and a bleating voice. Kepek talked to him in a strange language that Yerzhan didn't yet understand, but several times his uncle spoke a word that sounded like *talany*, 'from the steppe', and pointed to his nephew. Under Kepek's vigilant gaze, Petko first felt Yerzhan's hands, his upper arms and his shoulders, as if testing a stallion or a ram, then asked incomprehensible questions. Yerzhan tried to work out what he meant. It sounded like 'In the sky is the dance of the blind man'. Was this stranger asking after a song? But his uncle came to his rescue. 'What's your name?' Kepek translated Petko's question. 'Yerzhan,' Yerzhan replied. Petko's own trailer was at the end of the row. There the Bulgarian picked up Yerzhan's violin, sniffed at it and ran his tongue over the hairs of the bow. He burst into laughter and laughed for a long time while he cleaned the strings and bow with a bitter-smelling substance. Then he fetched wood resin and rubbed it over the bow in large movements and small circles by turn.

When he eventually started playing the violin, the sound was so pure that Yerzhan instantly realized the meaning of Petko's first comment: even a blind man would have seen the blue sky, the dance of the pure air, the clear sunlight, the snow-white clouds, the joyful birds.

It was his first lesson.

For the next four lessons Petko played his instrument without much explanation. Yerzhan copied the movements and memorized the black and white birds that sat on wires and were called 'notes' by Kepek. But Grandad Daulet soon became jealous. He recognized Yerzhan's progress on this new instrument. His grandson should learn the *dombra*, not the violin, and he decided to take the boy to Semey to show him the real master bards. They boarded a freight wagon that supplied bread to the stations along the branch line. At each stop, Tolegen, Grandad's friend, distributed frozen loaves. In the meantime, Daulet and Yerzhan lay on the thick sheepskin coats in the wagon's depths and stared at the forest of hands reaching for the bread when the train stopped. And when the train moved they stared at the snow-covered steppe whirling around them like a huge millstone sprinkled with flour.

And there, on the railway, where the telegraph poles raced backwards, Grandad and Tolegen waved their hands in the direction of the plain with the barbed wire, and Yerzhan again heard that clangorous, forgotten sound: Zone.

Once more, the buzzing gadfly began to circle above his consciousness. In the night he dreamt about it as a swarm of musical notes. By the morning, however, it had turned into a huge insect, circling above his head, before shamelessly descending upon his nose.

The old men were already drinking their tea with milk powder, dipping the crust of the last unsold loaf in their cups. The train clattered along the frozen rails. The fierce cold of the steppe blew in through the wagon door, which stood slightly ajar. But suddenly the shadows in the wagon shifted abruptly, as if pushed aside by the huge hairy legs of the fly on Yerzhan's nose. A din louder than its buzzing, worse than the rumble of the wagon and the empty metal bread boxes followed, penetrating the eardrums of the men and the boy. The wagon began to dance. The bread boxes began to dance. The old men disappeared through the open door. The fly made the ground under Yerzhan's feet spin. Then it dragged him into a rumbling darkness.

The Zone! That's how Yerzhan remembered that day, when the wagons toppled off the track and lay in the steppe. Eventually, a blood-drenched Grandad Daulet and Uncle Tolegen saved Yerzhan from darkness and the hairy fly's legs. They wrapped him in sheepskin while crying their miserly old men's tears.

So Yerzhan and his grandfather never made it to Semey. The boy was clearly not meant to learn from the great bard masters. They rode back to Kara-Shagan on a trolley that looked like a small locomotive. The steppe appeared sombre, just like the faces of the people. Leaden clouds swept across the sky without rain or snow. Hollow clouds, neither resounding with thunder nor flashing with lightning. It was strange how quickly these clouds raced across the sky when the air on the ground was so stagnant.

The next day they arrived home empty-handed, without gifts from the city. The people on the trolley gave them a few loaves of railway bread and a bag of Russian potatoes, before heading further into the steppe on their incomprehensible business. Several days passed before the sky brightened. No one went outside, except for Grandad Daulet, who had to attend to a rare passing train. They even peed into a copper bowl, which a swearing and cursing Kepek occasionally emptied out of the window.

Their urine – and especially Yerzhan's – turned red, as if from shame. The women, as usual, chattered about the end of the world. Grandad Daulet, when he wasn't asleep, spun the little dial on his radio, catching a squeak, a whistle, a hiss and some strange speech about an explosion.

They sat at home idly and didn't even let the boy play music. But eventually the two families gathered and Grandad Daulet slaughtered a ram. They cooked it, put on their festive clothes and ate the animal. After the feast, the old man released a mighty burp. He picked up one of the ram's bones and placed it on the city bride Baichichek's knees. 'Now show me,' he challenged Shaken, 'that you're still a bold young fellow!' Shaken rose from his seat and folded his hands behind his back. The old man tied them with a belt. Shaken walked up to his wife and, keeping his knees locked, bent down and grabbed the bone with his teeth. Everyone whooped with excitement. Afterwards Kepek lifted the bone from the knees of his silent sister, Kanyshat. And finally they placed the bone on the knees of three-year-old Aisulu and forced Yerzhan to bend for it. Both families cheered him on. Yerzhan had eaten a lot of dry meat that day and just as his teeth grabbed the bone, a deafening fart shook the house. Oh, how they laughed!

'A bomb!' Grandad Daulet yelled from beneath his wrinkles.

'Atomic!' Shaken, the scientist, added. 'We'll not only catch up with the Americans, we will surpass them!'

Kepek didn't pass up his chance for a witticism: 'The rocket's ready for take-off!'

And that's how they handled that explosion.

Yerzhan was a big boy now. And so when the summer came he was allowed to accompany Shaken to graze the herd. They went to the same river course where Grandad had once played the *dombra* for the boy. There the grass was still green. They tethered the horse to the base of a bush and stretched out on the ground, in the hope of feeling the water's coolness in the earth. The cattle wandered across the fresh expanse, unscorched by the sun. A moist scent hovered over the wide gully. After the naked sun of the steppe, fierce even in the mornings, the shade of the tamarisk and the saksaul bushes cooled the drops of sticky sweat on Uncle Shaken's and Yerzhan's hot faces. The dog, Kapty, ran about with his flame-hot tongue dangling, jostling the scattering herd back into a manageable bunch.

Eventually they left the herd to Kapty's enthusiastic supervision and mounted the horse and galloped down-stream towards the steppe surrounded by barbed wire. Uncle Shaken clearly knew the way, and the gullies and ravines brought them to the Zone that had tormented Yerzhan's boyish curiosity like a gadfly for all these years. Sitting behind Uncle Shaken, he gazed around eagerly, but the steppe looked just like the steppe: a small sun, as sharp as a nail, in a boundless, weary sky, scorched grassy stubble and stale, motionless air droning between them. Except that the earth here was a bit redder and the layer of dust under the horse's hooves was a bit thicker than usual.

They galloped for a long time. Shaken didn't speak, as if he was preoccupied listening to the sounds of the steppe. It wasn't until the sun appeared behind their backs that he suddenly said, 'Look, the goose…' Yerzhan leant out to the side, expecting to see wildlife, and maybe a lake. But ahead of them, stretching its concrete neck up out of the ground, stood a strange building. It looked like the ones Grandad had called 'elevators' when they were on Tolegen's train. In the distance Yerzhan could see other dark shapes.

As they came closer, the 'goose' appeared more like a crane, an immense concrete block half-crumpled, as if it had melted and run on one side. The boy gaped wide-eyed, but Uncle Shaken didn't linger here. He set the horse ambling towards the other structures. And soon Yerzhan could see them clearly: they were ruined houses.

The boy knew the ruins of Kazakh nomad halts and he had also seen graves in the steppe. They were rounded, as if time and nature had taken pity on them, carving away their corners and ledges bit by bit. The buildings here, on the other hand, seemed to have been casually smashed. Frames protruded at random angles through walls, walls jutted through roofs, roofs thrust down onto foundations. Yerzhan was terrified. Granny Ulbarsyn's end of the world had materialized in front of his eyes.

'Has Aisulu seen this?' he asked Uncle Shaken fearfully. The man shook his head. 'If we don't simply catch up with the Americans and then overtake them,' he added in his usual manner, 'the whole world will look like this!'

In the evenings, Grandad Daulet and Uncle Shaken often discussed the third world war that Shaken prepared for so assiduously at his work, while Yerzhan tried to fall asleep. But Uncle Shaken spoke loudly, broadcasting incomprehensible words to the world as if through a megaphone: 'The panic of pan-Americanism', 'The end of the world is proclaimed in this way' and 'Bombs will descend onto the earth, as if the fire of hell is poured forth'.

Perhaps it was these conversations, or perhaps it was Yerzhan's persistent fear of the Zone, or perhaps the sight of the dead town was the trigger, but from the day Yerzhan saw the goose and the ruins in the steppe, he dreamt about the imminent third world war over and over again. It usually happened out of the blue. Little planes appeared in a calm sky and attacked an American bomber. Or sometimes there was a night sky and stars chased around in all directions. But at the end the sky had always turned leaden-grey. A loud boom swept across the land, the cattle howled and a bright light lit up the world.

When it dispersed, a giant poisonous mushroom loomed over the earth like a djinn.

Shaken carried on like the radio: 'And the earth is the only thing we don't have to fear – there is no deception. As black as a mother in mourning, she will embrace everyone and take them into her barren and inflamed womb, which gave birth to them...'

'We are travellers, and the sky above us is full of enemy planes.'

As Yerzhan sank into sleep, he realized that Grandad Daulet and Uncle Shaken still hadn't finished discussing the imminent arrival of the third world war.

The train continued on across the endless Kazakh steppe, and the wires with their kestrels and jays, larks and rollers, and God only knows what other kinds of airborne wildlife, drifted after it from pole to pole, from pole to pole, like the notes of transcendental music shifting from beat to beat, from beat to beat. In a talkative mood now, my new companion had abandoned his commercial responsibilities and reached an understanding with the conductor that he was allowed to travel with me to his distant Semey. Life in the train and the carriage carried on as usual, with more and more new vendors, all of them women, selling camel wool, dried fish or simply pellets of dried sour milk. And in addition, they now occasionally offered picture postcards of naked, busty girls and bottles of the local beer, warm and frothy like urine. The old Kazakh in my compartment woke up but didn't turn towards us; he carried on grunting and wheezing, lying on his side, obviously listening with half an ear to what Yerzhan told me about his life.

We drank a glass of railway tea each – a favour from the conductor, who had acquired an extra cash-in-hand passenger. Then Yerzhan carried on with his story.

The boy progressed rapidly in his studies, not by the day, but by the hour, and not only in music, playing études by Kreutzer, Mazas and Rode before summer came, but also in the Russian language, albeit with a certain Bulgarian flavour, which had stayed with him to the present. Every now and then he would put in 'What do you think?', as if he were testing his listener's response. Although Kepek had noticed that Petko and Yerzhan could now manage perfectly well without his irrelevant and erratic translation, the uncle still contrived to interfere here and there. He held out his snotty handkerchief to his nephew and told him to put it under his chin – 'Pedo taught you to do that, didn't he?' – and grabbed the bow out of Yerzhan's hands during a break and tore off a snapped hair with special zeal. In any case, he never left his nephew alone with Petko in the trailer of the steppe Mobile Construction Unit.

The first phrases Yerzhan learnt in Russian were Petko's musical exclamations: 'Upper bow! Move the bow down! Third finger! Second string! Louder! Smooth movement!'

He dreamt these phrases, together with the sounds of the violin in different-coloured, rounded notes. His dreams had never been so jolly before. The notes walked about like little men. This one was fat and pompous, with a huge pot belly, while these minced along on skinny legs. And they fused together into bright pictures, like what happened when Yerzhan deliberately pressed on his eyes and multicoloured cabbages started blossoming under his fists. During the day he wanted to share these pictures that bloomed in his vision each night with his little girl-friend, Aisulu. So he stole up on her from behind and pressed her eyeballs in really firmly, intoning in a language she didn't understand, 'Whatnoteisthat? Sharpersound! Fingersfingersfingers! Where'sthebow? Nearerthebridge!'

On the long journey to the lessons, Yerzhan often asked his uncle, who had served in the Soviet Army, about this word or that in Russian, learning it off by heart, just in case. 'You're farting out of your arse!' Kepek taught the boy when he warmed up by practising his scales. And when he spotted in Yerzhan's pocket the metal box of rosin that Petko had put down just before they left, he asked, 'Why did you fucking nick that?' And so Yerzhan explained to Petko, 'I fucking nicked this,' as he returned the rosin and exclaimed, 'You're just farting out of your arse,' as he was asked to start the lesson with scales. Petko gazed at the boy admiringly, choking on his laughter as he repeated, 'You really take the biscuit, kid!'

Needless to say, the phrase was etched into Yerzhan's mind as the highest and most cheerful praise possible, and he patted his Aisulu on the back in exactly the same way: 'You really take the biscuit, kid!'

'Petko's no fool,' Shaken told the family after supper. He had taken Yerzhan to his violin lesson that day. After all, it was him who had bought the boy the violin, not Kepek. But instead of a lesson, Yerzhan was told to go away while Shaken chatted with Petko for over three hours. 'Petko graduated from the Moscow Conservatoire' – yet another incomprehensible word for Yerzhan's Russian musical vocabulary – Shaken continued to explain, 'where he studied with Oistrakh himself.' '*Oi, strakh!*' – 'Oh, terror!' in Russian – was what the city bride Baichichek cried out whenever she was frightened, and now too she seized the chance to spit and exclaim, '*Oi, strakh!*' 'He's no hotch-potch!' Shaken repeated, although he hadn't discovered how Petko had come to work at a Mobile Construction Unit just seven kilometres away from Kara-Shagan.

On their next trip to the lesson, Kepek merely gestured dismissively: 'Shaken knows fuck all!' Then he added, 'I, on the other hand, do know!' But then he fell silent and didn't reveal how Petko, whose name he couldn't even say properly, calling him 'Pedo, Pedo' all the time, had ended up here, in the middle of the Kazakh steppe.

*

One thing the Mobile Construction Unit had, however, and that was a shower. Even Grandad Daulet, who was secretly still peeved with the boy for betraying the *dombra* for the violin, decided to make the journey to a music lesson when he heard about the shower. Sweat flowed down his wrinkled neck and he gave off a sour smell as he rode towards the unit in the sweltering sun. Yerzhan sat behind him on the horse. Petko greeted them. He had combed his hair. He had tidied the trailer. The old man disappeared with his grandson behind the tarpaulin curtain. There Grandad massaged his own head with so much water and soap that it splashed everywhere and into Yerzhan's eyes too. But despite that, suddenly the boy saw the brown, wrinkled sac of Grandad's testicles peep out of the drawers which the old man had not taken off, even in the shower. 'Grandad, why have you got two balls?' Embarrassed, Daulet swiftly rearranged his clothing. 'Well, you see…' For a moment he hesitated, thinking about the question, then he said, 'I've got two children, that's why I've got two balls.'

'So has Shaken only got one, then?' the boy exclaimed in surprise. 'And does that mean Kepek hasn't got any?'

To these questions, however, Grandad couldn't think of a reply, so he merely shrugged his shoulders and grinned.

Grandad Daulet took a shine to Petko and in the early autumn he asked Kepek to invite the Bulgarian to join them on a fox hunt. Before Yerzhan was born, Daulet had raised a golden eagle for hunting. It died after Yerzhan's arrival and the hunting had stopped. Perhaps the old man felt that a new little eagle had hatched in his family and that the annual hunt in the reeds where Yerzhan was conceived had come to its natural end. Grandad Daulet now called his grandson a little eagle.

And so, in honour of the little eagle and his teacher, Grandad had decided to take the entire male population of Kara-Shagan out on a fox hunt. Uncle Kepek told Yerzhan how easily they used to hunt with the dog and the eagle. Kapty drove the fox out of its den and the eagle grabbed it from the air. But this time Grandad wanted to take the fox alive – the old-fashioned way. The arrangement was this: as soon as Kapty sniffed out a she-fox and drove it from its den, and the animal ran off in any direction, cunningly trying to confuse its tracks to distract the dog from its still-weak cubs, Grandad Daulet, Petko and Yerzhan would start driving the fox across the steppe with the low sun at their backs.

Uncle Shaken would be waiting for them just within shouting distance, and as soon as he spotted the animal he would dart out from the side and turn the direction of pursuit abruptly away from the sun: that is, he would force a *kaltarys* – a ninety-degree turn – on the fox. Then Uncle Kepek, also just within shouting distance, would take over. As soon as he spotted the fox, he would dart out on horseback from the side and turn the direction of Kapty's pursuit of the fox through another ninety degrees, so that the sun would be shining straight into the cunning she-fox's eyes. Meanwhile Grandad, Petko and the eagle-eyed Yerzhan, hallooing and whooping, would advance on their quarry, not from the side this time, but straight on, face to face, and… Yerzhan gave Grandad's double-barrelled shotgun a respectful glance.

Everything happened just as Grandad had planned. Kapty growled as he scrabbled the fox out of its den. The animal darted out, dashing off towards the sun, but Grandad started whooping so loudly that it stopped for a moment, then gathered its wits and dashed back past Kapty in the opposite direction – and the chase was on. Kapty galloped at full speed, with no breath left even to bark, but Grandad hallooed loud enough for the whole steppe to hear. Fortunately for Yerzhan, he was sitting behind Grandad's broad back, tied on with his belt, or he would certainly have gone deaf. Petko whooped too, sitting on a borrowed horse. This went on for about five minutes, until Grandad reined in his horse, and Yerzhan not only heard but actually saw Uncle Shaken give the fox that *kaltarys*, and it hurtled past to the side of them. Kapty stopped for a moment, but Grandad shouted to him, 'Crush it!' and Kapty finally barked at the top of his lungs and set off in the new direction.

While Shaken's voice and image shrank away, they galloped parallel with him, to take up their starting position for the *uluu kaltarys* – 'the main turn'. With his young eagle eyes, Yerzhan saw Shaken and Kepek intersect as two points off to the side. Then the picture vanished: Grandad Daulet had turned the horse. The noise of the chase approached a crescendo. 'Grandpa, let me see!' Yerzhan cried with all his might. Without taking off his belt, the old man swung the boy around and sat him on the saddle's front arch. He gently pulled the reins and the horse bent its head to one side, giving Yerzhan a full view of the steppe. And not without pride, the boy thought: This is probably how he treated his golden eagle.

Yerzhan could see no fox, but he saw Uncle Kepek, whooping as he rode along, and slightly ahead of him, he noticed the dog, Kapty, a faded fur ball. Closer and closer and closer… And suddenly Yerzhan became aware of a dusty point rushing towards them. 'Grandpa, look!' His heart pounded, caught between fervour and pity. Now Grandad would reach between stirrup leather and saddle girth, take out the gun and… But the old man froze, and then in the next moment whipped his horse, letting out a deafening ululation that merged with the whooping of Petko and Kepek. Grandad Daulet and Yerzhan now flew on their horse across the plain to meet the fox head on. It is rushing straight for us, fearing for its life, Yerzhan thought. But no. The fox, harried and confused, dropped in a dead faint on the ground and rolled head over heels, impelled by its own momentum. And before Kapty could gnaw through the animal's throat, Grandad Daulet cast his net and caught it. He did it so skilfully and accurately that the fox, still rolling, turned over twice and curled up in the net.

They had caught the fox alive – as men used to do in the olden days. Yerzhan saw the animal's defeated eyes full of anguish and despair. How had people managed to close off the free steppe on every side? And if it hadn't been for Petko, who refused Daulet's offer of a winter coat and begged him not to skin the animal, Kapty would have dug out her cubs too. The true goal isn't the goal, but the path to that goal, Petko said wisely. The old man had no choice but to agree with his guest. He sent the dog home with Uncle Kepek, waved his hand in frustration and released the bewildered fox back into the steppe.

Shaken had disappeared from sight as soon as the hunt was finished. Now he came riding towards them from the direction of the fox hole. Something was tucked under his sheepskin coat. When he reached the men he pulled out a fox cub. He said he'd caught it in the desert. It had probably run out in terror after its mother. Aisulu and Yerzhan can have a kitten! Yerzhan saw Petko's reproachful glance, but then he remembered how much Aisulu would like to have a fox cub, and he pretended not to have noticed Petko's glance.

Later that day, however, despite Petko's love of living creatures, Grandad Daulet slaughtered a ram in honour of their guest. He skinned it and cooked the head in a dish of noodles. Petko struggled to eat the meal with his hands. Under old Daulet's gaze, the violinist's delicate fingers were as limp as noodles themselves. After the hearty supper, Daulet picked up his *dombra* and sang one of his ancient songs for their guest, explaining to

Petko that here, as in the fox hunt, the listener is forced to follow the singer's twists and turns until he falls, like the fox, into the performer's snares.

> *There, in a world of shadows,*
> *Sadness has fled*
> *While in its stead,*
> *There's all that your heart may desire.*

'Let's turn ninety degrees,' the old man interjected, then continued:

> *Oh, the slippery world,*
> *Just like a torrent,*
> *Whirled us about like straw.*
> *Sweeping along,*
> *Spinning around*
> *Our hollow bodies.*

'And another ninety-degree turn,' exclaimed the old man, and waved his hand at Petko.

> *The world keeps on turning,*
> *Quietly murmuring,*
> *And pours into an eternal sea.*
> *Someone ahead,*
> *Someone behind,*
> *All are but straws in a bundle.*

'And now the final turn,' the old man roared, and finished his song in a hushed voice:

> *That peace is quiet,*
> *Calming and silent,*
> *The torrent fades into a backwater…*

As they sang, the fox cub, which had brought such joy to Aisulu, quietly slipped out of the house and was mauled to death by Kapty. They shed many tears as Uncle Kepek buried the furry little body off in the distance. From that evening on, each night, Yerzhan would hear a howl when the mother fox came to their door and begged for her cub. Kapty never barked when she came. Instead he would whine, as he did before an atomic blast.

That autumn an entire new window into the world opened up for the two-family population of Kara-Shagan. The city bride Baichichek insisted that Shaken went into town to buy a new radio with a gramophone attached. This was a genuine radiogram – nothing at all like Grandad's hoarse, husky old Strela. From now on the days were structured. In the mornings Shaken exercised, encouraged by the trainer Gordeev and the pianist Potapov for everyone to hear. Then it was Grandad Daulet's turn as he and the freshly exercised Shaken listened to the latest news that came after the Soviet anthem and Shaken's unvarying credo: 'We will not merely catch up with America, but overtake it!' And when Grandad Daulet had to tend his tracks, the women listened to the radio dramas on the second Kazakhstan channel. And when the women went to milk the cows and collect brushwood in the steppe, Kepek nestled up against the radiogram. He stuck various wires into it and tuned in to demoniacal music that set him shaking and twitching even without any drink.

Kind-hearted Petko gave Yerzhan two records: *Lendik Kogam* – Leonid Kogan – and *Dinrit* – Dean Reed. *Lendik Kogam* played the violin so beautifully, as if Petko had decided not to get distracted by any more pupils and simply play on his own. And *Dinrit* sang songs that sounded just like the ones Kepek fished for with his wires, only they possessed the same purity and exceptional joy as *Lendik Kogam*. Yerzhan and Aisulu played these two records over and over again, until the grown-ups showed up and put the records back on the shelves and the children to bed.

For anyone who has never lived in the steppe, it is hard to understand how it is possible to exist surrounded by this wilderness on all sides. But those who have lived here since time out of mind know how rich and variable the steppe is. How multicoloured the sky above. How fluid the air all around. How varied the plants. How innumerable the animals in it and above it. A dust storm can spring up out of nowhere. A yellow whirlwind can suddenly start twirling round the air in the distance in the same way that women spin camel wool into twine. The entire, imponderable weight of that immense, heavy sky can suddenly whistle across the becalmed, submissive land...

As he grew, Yerzhan noticed all the subtle shades and gradations of the road they followed to Petko's music lessons. And that road seemed like music to him: it was just as fluent, the sounds were just as varied. The notes of the wind swayed on the little tamarisk and saltwort shrubs. Shrews and ground squirrels sang the second and third voices.

At home, Grandad's severe, wrinkled face seemed to the boy like the Bach violin concerto that he was learning to play. Shaken's tedious cheerfulness was like Kreisler's *Miniature Viennese March*, which they had decided not to bother learning at all. Kepek's dumb behaviour was like Gaviniès's endless études. And his Aisulu's pink-cheeked little face was Vivaldi's *Winter*, which the Bulgarian Petko played with ecstatic gusto during the late Kazakh summer.

And only the women, including the city bride Baichichek, did Yerzhan still associate with the monotonous sounds of the old-fashioned *dombra*.

The joy of the steppe, the joy of music and the joy of childhood always coexisted in Yerzhan with the anticipation of that inescapable, terrible, abominable thing that came as a rumbling and a trembling, and then a swirling, sweeping tornado from the Zone. At such times Uncle Shaken was usually away on his work shift. But on the rare occasions when he was at home, he, Grandad Daulet and Uncle Kepek argued non-stop while they were locked inside with the families for several days. Shaken, who was blamed for everything that was happening, lit up like the steppe itself when there was a blast. He preached to the others that it was more than just an atom bomb. It was our Soviet response to the arms race, without which we would all have been gone a long time ago. But the blasts were necessary for peaceful purposes too. In order to build communism! 'It is our absolute duty not merely to catch up with, but to overtake the Americans! In case there's a third world war!' he concluded with his hallmark phrase. 'Stop giving us the propaganda line!' Grandad replied, equally heated. He had fought in both world wars: in the first he dug trenches in the rear and in the second he had reached the Elbe on foot, and fraternized with the Americans there. 'There's nothing in the world worth fighting a war for! I understand the railway, it transports people and cargo – that's good for everyone! But what good does your atom-schmatom do? You've turned the entire steppe into a desert! You never see a gerbil or a fox!'

'And the menfolk can't get it up any more!' Kepek intervened with an incomprehensible assertion of his own, which made Shaken look away shamefacedly.

One day in late autumn, after one of these periods of incarceration with long arguments, Shaken went to the city and brought a television back home. 'If I can't do it, let this educate you!' he announced.

With the arrival of the television in Uncle Shaken's house, the radiogram spontaneously migrated to Grandad Daulet's, and now Dean Reed, backed up by red-cheeked Aisulu's 'Liza, Liza, Liza, Lizabet', sang out fearlessly for Yerzhan alone. Moreover, Yerzhan's and Aisulu's days were now clearly divided into daytime and evening. The daytime, which had to be survived – with the music, with Dean Reed, with running around the steppe, with forays to the wagons on the siding, with absolutely anything. And the evening time, which had to be reached in order to immerse oneself, like sinking into sleep, in that little television, with its alluring blue glow in the early autumn or winter darkness. Cartoons, concerts, films, the television news and especially the music which started the main news. Shaken called the news music 'Forward, Time!' as proudly as if he had composed it himself. Yerzhan and Aisulu never missed a single programme until they fell asleep, exhausted, right there in front of the television, collapsing on the felt rug.

And then on New Year's Eve Dean Reed himself appeared on the 'Blue Light' programme. He looked exactly like he did on the sleeve of his record – tall, slim and handsome. And what's more, as if he knew Aisulu's secret request, he started singing her favourite song, 'Liza, Liza, Liza, Lizabet'. After that, whenever Yerzhan started playing his violin, picking out either Kogan or Dean Reed, he tied his mother's black silk scarf round his neck as his bow tie. Like Dean Reed.

He knew for certain who he was going to look like when he grew up.

*

How Yerzhan yearned to look like Dean Reed! In his dreams he saw himself with the same kind of handsome features and long hair. But not only in his dreams! Even when he was wide awake he imagined that he was this good-looking American man. Especially when he watched his own lengthening shadow. He held his violin like a guitar and twirled round so that his shadow squirmed about on the ground. 'We've got to keep searching, searching, she'll be by my side, follow the sun...' He got so used to his image that when he happened to glance by chance into his mother's mirror, he was dumbfounded at the sight of his own face, expecting to see the face printed on the sleeve of the LP.

Thanks to Grandad Daulet, Yerzhan had learnt to play the *dombra*; thanks to Uncle Shaken he had encountered the violin; thanks to Uncle Kepek he had acquired his teacher, Petko; thanks to Petko he had learnt music and Russian and even acquired Dean Reed. And thanks to Dean Reed he had learnt to read, since he wanted to find out everything about this tall, handsome, happy man. Now Uncle Shaken would often bring back newspapers and magazines from the city for him, *Rovesnik* – My Age – or *Krugozor* – Outlook. And from them Yerzhan learnt, letter by letter, about the life of his idol. 'Maria, Maria, Maria,' Yerzhan chirped on his camel. 'Bam bam bamba' Petko heard the boy sing, and filled in the gaps in Yerzhan's knowledge about Dean Reed, whom he had seen once in a Moscow television studio. Yerzhan was enraptured by these stories, but he didn't show it. After all, he already knew how jealous Grandad was of his violin. So if Petko ever found out from Uncle Kepek that Yerzhan at home dropped his bow and grabbed his violin like a guitar to make his lengthening shadow look like Dean Reed, how jealous would the teacher be!

Not much troubled Yerzhan in those days. There were of course the explosions in the Zone, which the boy never called by their proper name out of visceral fear. But besides that he had only one other worry: which side in the third world war would Dean Reed be on? With his head full of the constant arguments between Shaken and Grandad Daulet about the imminent third world war and his nightmares of little silver planes suddenly turning into iron eagles and diving at him as if he were a fox cub, running across the steppe, unable to find a burrow or any kind of refuge from the rumbling, or the darkening sky, or the new sun rising in the black sky, or the mushroom hanging over the steppe, Yerzhan would wake soaked in sweat, curled up tight like a fox cub, and think in horror, afraid to move: Which side was Dean Reed on?

Who could he tell about these nocturnal fears? Petko and all the others believed he was a faithful disciple of Leonid Kogan. So with whom could he share his torments about Dean Reed?

*

'Wunderkind!' Petko said one day, gazing at Yerzhan with loving eyes, and the nickname stuck firmly. Uncle Kepek adopted it promptly and Shaken exclaimed, 'Now we will definitely not only catch up with but also overtake America!' He explained what the word meant in translation from the German. '*Wunder*' was a miracle and '*Kinder*' was a child, and so he surmised that it would be more correct to say '*Wunderkinder*'. Grandad Daulet learnt this word too. Only the grannies Kazakhized it, calling their grandson '*buldur kimdir*' – 'this someone'. Yerzhan liked his new nickname and flaunted it at every opportunity: when Grandad's friend Tolegen came on the delivery train, when a passenger train stopped in the siding, when the local militiaman or the district doctor came to see Petko at the Mobile Construction Unit. One of the adults would cry, 'Wunderkind!' and Yerzhan would immediately grab his violin and rush to answer the call, playing Paganini's *Caprice* or Vivaldi's *Spring*.

'A wunderkind!' they all agreed – the idle passengers in the train, the terrifying militiaman and the doctor, and kind old Uncle Tolegen too.

'We have to show him to the conservatoire!' Shaken enthused. 'I'll take a few days' leave and go to Almaty with him!' Yerzhan was terrified. Did they want to conserve him? Is that what they did with a wunderkind – like fruit in jam and cucumbers in brine? Shaken explained what the conservatoire was, but it didn't calm Yerzhan. He still remembered what had happened last time when Grandad Daulet wanted to take him to the city and the fly started buzzing in his ear and the wagon tumbled over. Luckily, except for Uncle Shaken, everyone else seemed to be on Yerzhan's side. Grandad dismissed the idea with a shrug: 'He'll go to school soon and it will all blow over!' – as if he was talking about a brief cold. Uncle Kepek shrugged the conservatoire idea off from a different angle: 'Even if he is a paedo, our Pedo studied with Oistrakh!' – and he pointed at people playing the violin or the *dombra* on the television. 'Look, my little darling nephew plays a hundred times better than any of those blockheads! Give me two strings, put a stick in my hand and I'm the master of the land!' The comment made Grandad angry, but it didn't make him change his mind.

'Hey, Wunderkind, come here and give my bumps a rub!' Granny Ulbarsyn called from the next room. She certainly wouldn't let her favourite masseur go anywhere.

Yerzhan went to school when he was seven. 'Went' sounds very simple, but the school was in a village eight kilometres from Kara-Shagan, so 'going to school' meant walking eight kilometres in one direction and eight kilometres back. On the first day, Grandad insisted that Yerzhan hang the *dombra* from one shoulder and the violin from the other. At school the pupils gathered in the sports hall and Yerzhan played first one instrument and then the other. Since that day no more coaxing was required for the nickname 'Wunderkind' to migrate from Kara-Shagan to school, and his classmates soon started to call Yerzhan 'Wunda'. And 'Wunda' played Kurmangazy and Tchaikovsky by turns whenever the school inspectors came to visit.

Winter arrived. Howling hungry wolves and jackals loped across the steppe. It was no longer safe for Yerzhan to walk to school and so Grandad took him by horse. The boy warmed up in the classroom, while Grandad Daulet sat in the railway canteen. His patience lasted for two days. Then he informed the director of the school that he would take his grandson home for the rest of the winter. And once again Yerzhan was left alone with his violin, exercise books and pencils.

Under the dim light of the lamp Granny Ulbarsyn sorted through camel wool while Yerzhan hunched over the table and drew whatever came to his mind. And as the long winter evenings dragged on, he eventually taught his Aisulu to read and write. She started school the following summer and quickly became the best pupil in the class, because she knew in advance what the other untutored children were only just trying to master.

Uncle Shaken now took them to school on the camel, crammed in between the two humps. But when he disappeared to work his shift catching up with and overtaking the Americans, Grandad Daulet sat them both on the donkey. He handed them each a dry cob of maize to scatter the grains along the route. 'That way,' he said, 'you won't get lost... And if you do get lost,' he added slyly, 'we'll set the chickens on the trail and they'll find you.' Although how could they get lost, when the route ran alongside the railway line the whole time? And in the mornings, on their way to school, the sun shone in their faces from the right all the time and in the afternoon, on their way home, it would shine on their right side again.

Aisulu held on tight to Yerzhan's thin shoulders and they galloped, sometimes with the wind, sometimes against it, sometimes through a whirlwind, sometimes through a dust storm. And in the early days they wasted their time vainly scattering grains of maize, which the skylarks and rollers of the steppe religiously pecked up. But soon the sun hid behind the fast-moving autumn clouds.

Aisulu was still joyfully singing a Dean Reed song right in Yerzhan's ear when their donkey picked up a cabbage stalk thrown out of a passenger train. The animal swallowed the stalk whole and immediately choked. It lashed out so suddenly that Aisulu tumbled off the donkey's back in mid-note. Then Yerzhan followed, to the other side. The animal shuddered and wheezed and shook its head from side to side. Yerzhan didn't lose time and jumped up and flung himself at the donkey in a fury. At first he was going to beat it, but when he saw the foam frothing out of its mouth, he was seriously frightened. The animal wouldn't let him get close; it kicked out and lashed at him with its tail, baring its teeth and snorting terribly. 'Hold him!' Yerzhan shouted, and little Aisulu, dropping her briefcase on the ground, grabbed the reins and pulled the donkey's head down towards the ground. Without stopping to think, Yerzhan parted its jaws and stuck his arm up to the elbow into its mouth, reaching through the foamy mush. His fingernails touched the stalk and with all his strength the boy jerked it out. The donkey howled and sank its teeth into Yerzhan's arm. Swearing like a grown-up, Yerzhan shrieked, 'Fuck your mother!' But he didn't let go of the stalk and pulled it out of the donkey's jaws. He ignored his bleeding arm and smacked the animal between the eyes! The donkey howled in resentful gratitude at the top of its lungs: 'Ee-yaw! Ee-ee-yaw! Ee-ee-ya-aw!' Aisulu, too, swore just like Granny Sholpan: 'A plague on you! Foul beast! Do you hear what I say?' And then without any more lamentations she took the scarf off her head, licked away the blood flowing along Yerzhan's arm from under the hoisted-up sleeve and bound the wound tightly.

On that day they missed school.

Yerzhan and Aisulu shared happy childhood years. Together they plastered the back walls of the two houses with cowpats that were their fuel for the winter. Or they hunted through the goods trains that had stopped on the siding. And sometimes, when a wagon was piled up with coal, they swept out a sack or two of the dust that was stuck along the side frames of the bogies or over the suspension of the wheels. Or they managed to break out a wooden brace that stabilized the platform, to use as firewood or building material. But what they enjoyed most was to take hot water and powdered milk to passenger trains waiting in the siding for an express goods train with important cargo to pass and sell their beverage or play the *dombra* to earn a little money. And city people from unknown lands, golden-toothed Uzbeks, yellow-haired Russians and red-shirted Gypsies gave them brand-new coins and paper roubles. And sometimes they would even receive a sweet or some city knick-knack. And once someone gave them a bar of chocolate. They shared the sweets half-and-half, but Yerzhan generously let Aisulu have all the knick-knacks, and she accumulated a whole heap of them in boxes and little drawers: lipstick, Komsomol and Young Pioneer badges, one ballpoint pen, a key ring and even a huge pair of sunglasses.

Of course, it was rare for passenger trains to wait here; mostly they were goods trains, some with cement, some with timber where they could strip the bark, some with sand, some with china clay that they could chew instead of black tar.

But at least once a week Uncle Tolegen's wagon, coupled to a goods train, travelled round all these way stations that were called 'spots', bringing them railway bread and occasionally flour for round bread rolls, sugar, salt and tea bricks. The grown-ups, however, went out to meet that wagon themselves.

*

It wasn't long before Aisulu started to accompany Yerzhan to his lessons with Petko, with firm instructions from Uncle Kepek not to get separated for a single moment. Unfortunately, Petko's Mobile Construction Unit lay in a completely different direction from the school: if you drew a triangle connecting home, school and Petko, then Petko was right up at the apex. One afternoon, after Yerzhan had played yet another Mozart march on the violin for the school assembly and they were running late, the children decided not to go home but to head straight to Petko. They wanted to try a new route. Using Grandad Daulet's method, Yerzhan calculated that if the sun shone into their right eye on the way from home to school, then now, in Kepek's Russian expression, it should shine 'right up their arse'.

The steppe lay all around them, like a wide-open eye, mutely escorting them on their way, and an equally huge, bright eye watched them from above. Ensconced on the donkey, they weren't frightened – no snake or steppe spider would bite them, no fox or kite would come close. Small black spots of occasional graves jutted up out of the horizon like markers indicating their route.

But suddenly one of these spots started to move. Yerzhan quickly realized that it was a solitary wolf who had come out on his pre-winter hunt. He was lurking in the steppe waiting for prey. The boy had learnt what to do. He took off his school jumper and wound it round his hand like a flag. He lashed the donkey and waved the flag, whooping at the top of his voice. He didn't ask Aisulu to follow his example, but she imitated him straight away, whirling her jumper about and lashing the donkey with it, while squealing so shrilly that Yerzhan was almost deafened. The wolf had not expected such a show. Surprised by the ambush, he turned and took to his heels, running ahead in the same direction as the donkey. Inadvertently the children found themselves in pursuit of the animal. They galloped for almost half an hour. Then all at once the wolf disappeared and at long last they saw the trailers and the excavators. They had reached Petko safely.

They didn't mention their adventure to the violin teacher and without any delay the lesson began. Petko taught Yerzhan, and Yerzhan almost simultaneously passed on what he had learnt to Aisulu, who didn't know Russian and couldn't read music yet, and only annoyed Petko. But as soon as rain started falling outside, the air inside the trailer cleared too. And when the rain turned into a thunderstorm, the teacher and his pupils had to stop playing in order to save the donkey. The animal was so terrified that it had broken free and was now soaked right down to the very last hair on its short tail.

The rain and the thunder carried on into the evening. There was inky blackness on all sides. And, of course, going home was completely out of the question. That night they missed their indispensable television viewing and stayed in Petko's trailer.

*

Aisulu and Yerzhan shared a bed. The girl soon drifted off. The boy, on the other hand, couldn't sleep. As midnight approached he heard the wind howling and the rain lashing at the little trailer. And then he sensed eyes in the darkness. He looked around frightened and saw Petko standing beside their bed. Although the night was as black as pitch, Yerzhan felt the full force of the man's gaze and lay very still, more dead than alive, not knowing what to expect and more afraid for Aisulu than for himself. But Petko must have become aware of the boy staring back at him, because he awkwardly busied himself adjusting the blanket that had slipped off. Yerzhan's heart pounded hollowly and Petko's keen musical ear caught the echoing rhythm of childish fear. He sat down on the edge of the bed, stroked Yerzhan's head and said, 'Sleep. Don't be afraid, I'm here...' Then he added, 'Would you like me to tell you a story about an Eternal Boy?'

And without waiting for a reply he started whispering: 'A long, long time ago there was a boy called Wolfgang. Do you know what that name means? Walking wolf.' Yerzhan shuddered at that – perhaps it was cunning Petko who had sent the wolf into the steppe? 'This boy was such a talented musician that he could play any instrument with his eyes blindfolded. One night, when Wolfgang couldn't sleep and picked out notes for his music from among the stars, the silver-faced moon climbed down from the sky and started dancing, enticing him to follow her outside into the street, along the river, to the lake. The music of this dance was so entrancing that the boy followed the moon on and on, unable to gather his wits or resist. The moon walked across the water, luring him ever further with her song. The boy followed her, and where the moon left only a shimmering silvery trail, full of magical sounds, the boy sank deeper and deeper into the water. His weightless soul seemed to be flying after the moon, but his body walked as if it was chained to the earthly paths of the wolf. The music sounded duller and duller, the water grew deeper and deeper above and around him. And then, finally, the silvery thread of music broke off. The eternal silence of silt and the lake bottom filled the boy's ears and all the spaces of his body, and with his final breath he howled like a wolf...

'The boy was saved – maybe by people, maybe by water nymphs, maybe by elves. His body continued to live and grew, but his soul stayed there in that night, at that lake, enchanted for ever by the moon and her silvery trail, full of music and dancing... And you remind me of that eternal boy,' Petko finished, or perhaps Yerzhan was already dreaming and it wasn't Petko's words, but the rustling of the silvery rain outside the window bringing this sweet and terrible tale to an end.

The next morning the thunderstorm had ceased, but the rain kept on and on. And the steppe was so wet and muddy that no donkey could have gone even two steps. Petko's work had also been brought to a standstill by the weather, so after eating breakfast they took up the violin again and worked on Bohm and Handel by turns.

The day passed and evening came, but the rain didn't stop. How could they know that all this time Grandad Daulet, who had left his son Kepek on the tracks, and Shaken, who was out of his mind with worry over his only daughter, were galloping – one on a horse and one on a camel – round the houses of Yerzhan's and Aisulu's classmates, and couldn't find them anywhere.

Yerzhan and Aisulu returned home on the third day in the guilty sunshine on the cheerful donkey that had caught up on its sleep. The girl was greeted with fervent hugs, while Yerzhan encountered the whip. And Uncle Kepek pestered both of them with strange questions.

They continued to skip classes on especially blizzardy days. Yerzhan taught Aisulu music and counting and writing at home. And after the second school winter he decided that he should stay back in the second class for a year, so that Aisulu could catch up with him, and then they would sit at the same desk for the rest of their lives. And although Yerzhan not only played music better than all the others but also read and counted and drew better than everyone else in his class, when spring came he suddenly forgot his text-books at home, or didn't remember his homework, blaming it on the music, or simply drew blots in his exercise book.

The teachers tried to summon his parents to school, but Yerzhan didn't pass on their messages. He knew the teachers wouldn't travel eight kilometres there and eight back to complain about his poor progress. And so he was kept back in the second school year. When Grandad found out, he wanted to whip his grandson again, but Granny Ulbarsyn interceded. She blamed the music. The music had completely worn the poor boy out. But to be on the safe side, she nevertheless sent Yerzhan to stay with Granny Sholpan for a few days. Granny Sholpan was delighted and said that while her son-in-law Shaken was at his shift, Yerzhan would be the man of the house.

And so, in the torrid heat Yerzhan drove the herd to the distant river meadow in the gullies, to the river that had dried up for the summer. There, among the stones and the sand, the herd sought out rare wisps of steppe grass and turned over boulders with their horns to lick the residual moisture off the undersides.

The naked sun beat down pitilessly on the boy's head and neither the scorched, lifeless tamarisk bushes nor the crooked-armed saksaul offered any shelter. Yerzhan tied his T-shirt round his head. But the rest of his body burnt in the ferocious sun. Eventually the heat became unbearable and he cautiously rinsed off his skin with heated water from Shaken's army flask. Then he let a blissful sheep lick the moisture off his skin. The animal's rough tongue soothed the midday itch.

In the evening he returned sunburnt to Granny Sholpan's house. The old woman and her granddaughter smeared sour milk over the boy's back and chest. And life returned to Yerzhan's body under Aisulu's soft little palms.

*

Yerzhan started the second class for the second time. This time, however, he shared a desk with Aisulu. They competed for As in their studies and the teachers were overjoyed, as they believed that Aisulu's mentorship of the failing student had worked. How could any of them know that at home it was Yerzhan who took control of the lessons? He produced two copies of all the drawings, and gave the good ones to Aisulu and kept the rough drafts for himself. He solved the difficult maths problems and told her the right spellings in dictation. Since he was taller and stronger than all these small fries by a whole year, he also stood up for Aisulu and wouldn't let anyone hurt her.

It was during a Kazakh-language lesson that the classroom windows started to jangle and benches shifted about on the floor. The blackboard crashed down off the wall and trapped their terrified teacher, lame-legged Kymbat. Yerzhan dashed forwards and rescued her. Then he ordered his classmates to crawl underneath their desks. A rumbling ran through the ground again. He broke out a window. His hand bled but he ignored the cut and dragged Aisulu into the open. A humming blast of air zoomed past and the tiles of the school roof came tumbling down.

And then suddenly an appalling silence. No sheep bleating, no dogs barking and no donkeys braying – even the ubiquitous flies had stopped buzzing. There was only Aisulu, lying face down in the dust, whispering her prayers – in the name of Allah, the most Merciful.

*

Later that autumn, as if this terrifying blast had never happened, or perhaps precisely because of it, the school bus headed over potholed, dusty roads towards the atomic workers' town. Aisulu's father, Shaken, had organized a school trip for their class to see his place of work. The bus journey took a day. They stayed overnight in the sports hall of the local school and in the morning the children were taken, freshly washed and de-dusted, to the 'experimental reactor'. In the information room, Yerzhan and Aisulu played a duet for the workers on their instruments. Then they were shown a film about the peaceful use of nuclear power. Some of the children had never watched a film before and the rustling of the sound and the quick scene changes frightened them and they cried. After the film Uncle Shaken, dressed in a white coat and white hat, like all the other workers, appeared and announced that this was the place where they were doing absolutely everything possible not only to catch up with but also to overtake America. He showed them different-coloured balls on a thick wire and set out to explain to them what he called a 'chain reaction'. There were two sets of balls on either end of the wire. Shaken took a ball from one group and used it to knock another ball just like the first one out of the other group, setting the first ball in the place of the one that had flown out. Yerzhan wanted to laugh out loud. Did they really have to be brought all this way to be taught playing tag with balls? But Aisulu watched wide-eyed, trying as hard as she could to memorize everything her father said. She even asked him questions, talking to him like some stranger, not her father, addressing him as Shaken Nurpeisovich.

A second film followed about an atomic explosion. And then finally the fun started. In the playground they were handed gas masks and chased after each other like aliens. But sadly the fun didn't last long. Because suddenly a real alien in a big rubber suit broke into their group. And everyone froze. He made a beeline for Aisulu. He grabbed her with his claw gloves. She screamed. And she screamed so loud that even through her gas mask and his gas mask Yerzhan could hear her cry for help. He ran towards her. But before he had reached them, the alien let go of Aisulu and lifted his helmet. It was Uncle Shaken, laughing out loud. Aisulu immediately joined in with her father's laughter. Only Yerzhan looked at him horrified. A strange tremble had seized him from inside.

Towards evening Uncle Shaken took the children to the Dead Lake. 'Don't drink the water and do not touch it,' he told them. It was a beautiful lake that had formed after the explosion of an atomic bomb. A fairy-tale lake, right there in the middle of the flat, level steppe, a stretch of emerald-green water, reflecting the rare stray cloud. No movement, no waves, no ripples, no trembling – a bottle-green, glassy surface with only cautious reflections of the boys' and girls' faces as they peeped at its bottom by the shore. Could there possibly be some fairy-tale fish or monster of the deep to be found in this static, dense water?

The bus driver called Uncle Shaken to help him with a punctured tyre. Yerzhan was left in charge of the class. He saw his long shadow reflected on the water's surface. Dean Reed in the boundless steppe, underneath the limitless sky, above the bottomless water. He briefly took Aisulu's hand. Then he let go of it and pulled off his T-shirt and trousers and walked calmly into the forbidden water. For a moment he splashed about in it and then, to the admiring and terrified twittering of Aisulu and the others, he walked out of the water, shook himself off as if nothing had happened and dressed again in his canvas trousers and Chinese T-shirt.

Nobody snitched on him. And for a long time afterwards everyone recalled with respectful admiration Wunda's dramatic escapade.

Part Two

Do La
The Destiny

The train moved on across the steppe like Yerzhan's story – without stopping, without hesitating, onwards and forwards. It was strange, but in this story there was none of that bitterness reminiscent of the old steam trains, which blew their nasty smoke into the last carriages on the bends. No, the diesel locomotive drew the train along without any strain, smoothly and unfalteringly.

Those childhood years were like a blue-and-yellow happiness, growing between the sky and the earth. But still the fear that something could happen at any moment, pouncing with a sudden roar and tearing the tiles off the roof, stayed with Yerzhan for the next two or three years. Everything seemed to be going as it should: autumns in school were followed by ferocious winters, when their door was piled so high with snow that there was nothing else to do but play on the violin or the *dombra*. Sometimes the boy had to climb out through the little window at the side of the house to scrape away the snowdrifts with their only railway spade.

After the musical winter came the no less musical spring, when the songs poured out of him. He and Aisulu followed their bidding, riding not off to school on the donkey, but towards the hills, where fields of scarlet tulips blossomed in a blaze of swaying notes.

And after that summer itself started imperceptibly blazing – without any school, thank God, but again with music, and with the herd and a separation in the afternoon. After all, he couldn't take thin-skinned Aisulu with him in the scorching heat, could he!

And the thing that loomed over him like a visceral fear could happen in the middle of the sweltering summer, when sheep suddenly started bleating as if they were under the knife and went dashing in all directions, cows dug their horns into the ground and the donkey squealed and rolled around in the dust... And a slight rumble would run through the ground, Yerzhan's legs would start trembling, and then his whole body, and the fear would rise up from his shaking knees to his stomach and freeze there in a heavy ache, until the sky cracked over his head and shattered into pieces, crushing him completely, reducing him to dust, to sand, to scraps of grass and wool. And the black whirlwind hurtled past above him with a wild howl.

It happened in winter, and at night, and in autumn, and in the morning, and in the music, and in a pause in the music – without any regularity or forewarning: it could always happen, at any moment, hanging over his head as implacably as fear itself, as the future.

*

And *it* happened when Yerzhan was twelve years old and Aisulu was eleven. It was in the fifth class at school, after the long winter holidays. First the girls and then the boys in their class started to outgrow Yerzhan. But, after all, he was a year older than them, and he had always been taller and stronger. At first the difference wasn't very noticeable: so what if Serik or Berik had stretched out a bit, that didn't make them any brighter! But when Aisulu, his little mite Sulu, his slim-winged swallow Sulu, started overtaking Yerzhan, he sensed that something was wrong. The same fear that had always begun with a trembling in his knees and frozen as a heavy ache in his stomach seemed to have risen higher now, right up to his throat – and got stuck there, preventing his body from growing.

In the mornings, Yerzhan did pull-ups on the door frame. He nailed a rusty wheel hoop to the back wall of the house. From television he knew that basketball players grew taller than anyone else and in secret, when no one watched, he jumped up to the hoop for hours, tossing whatever he could find through it – a bundle of rags or a ball of camel wool. And at night he stretched in bed, imagining that he would wake up in the morning as Dean Reed. But he had stopped growing.

Other people noticed it too and wanted to help. Granny Ulbarsyn fed him with the livers of newborn spring lambs, Grandad Daulet ordered carrots from the city through his friend Tolegen, and Uncle Shaken brought disgusting fish oil back from his shift. But that only produced a foul-smelling burp! Yerzhan ate it all. But he had stopped growing.

He gave up music. In any case, Petko had gone back to Bulgaria, where a family member had died. And Yerzhan spent the whole summer hiding away with his herd in the gullies close to the Zone. He lay on the ground naked for withering days on end in the hope that the sun would help. But even the heat made no difference. He had stopped growing.

And one day his faithful and obedient donkey brought him back to the house half-dead from the bite of a camel spider.

On 1 September that year Yerzhan did not go to school. Uncle Shaken took Sulu, all dressed up, on her own. On 2 September the two grannies persuaded the boy to stand in for Shaken, who had had to leave urgently for his shift. 'At least escort her,' they said, 'even if you don't sit through lessons.' Grandad Daulet, however, told Yerzhan not to come back home unless he had done his schoolwork. Yerzhan accompanied Aisulu but refused to sit on the donkey with the towering girl and followed the animal at a distance. In the quiet autumn steppe Sulu started singing. It wasn't Dean Reed. It was the sad song of Abai, who once lived in this steppe:

> *Entering into my ears, flooding through my full height,*
> *The harmonious sound and sweet refrain*
> *Awaken many feelings in my heart.*
> *If you would love, then love as I...*

The world does grow in secret from a thought,
And I nourish myself with hopes.
Now my sly soul understands
And my heart throbs inside my body...

Yerzhan picked up on only two words in this song: 'height' and 'body'...

He sat through lessons that day, at the desk right at the back, on his own, not going out for any breaks, and pretended to be asleep when Sulu came to the window. After school boys and girls set off back home in pairs. Yerzhan walked in front of the donkey, not glancing round at sad, silent Aisulu. He so badly wanted her assurances that no matter what was wrong and no matter what happened to him, she would still love no one but him and marry no one but him, as she had promised in their childhood. On the other hand, he realized that she was almost half a head taller than him, and if *it* carried on... He couldn't think beyond that; he was overwhelmed, not by the usual fear, but by a rage that took its place, rising up from his trembling knees, through his hot stomach, to his heavy, throbbing head: he wanted to kill himself, to kill her, towering up on that bad-tempered, noisy donkey; he wanted to smash this railway, grind it to dust, and this earth, and this sky...

*

In this state of mind he went to school for another two or three weeks, or perhaps even longer. Every day he witnessed the inevitable but refused to accept it: the children around him were growing by the hour. And his Aisulu was blossoming into a gorgeous beauty before his very eyes. Girls and boys swirled round her like the little stars in the sky round the full moon, and only Yerzhan sat in the corner during breaks, with a face like grey earth, dropping his heavy head on the desk and glancing out from under his brows at the smile on her face or the joyful response to it from some Serik or Berik.

Kill her! Kill myself! The thoughts pounded in time with his heart as it beat faster and faster, and again he plodded away after classes, immersed in his own agonizing doubts, which never led to anything or any place except home.

On one of these days he didn't go to school, using the excuse that he was ill, and since Uncle Shaken was still on his shift, Uncle Kepek took Aisulu to school on the same tireless donkey. All day long Yerzhan roasted in the flames of his own thoughts and towards evening, at the time when Aisulu usually came home, he walked out of the house. And the first image he became aware of was his own uncle, Kepek, riding on the donkey with Aisulu. She sat in front of him instead of behind, so that his arms were around her youthful body as he was holding the reins, and she was quietly singing one of her tender songs, something like Dean Reed's 'Come with Us'…

Yerzhan didn't greet them. And at night he burnt, not in an imaginary blaze but in the genuine infernal fever of his own boyish hell.

Granny Ulbarsyn took him to the local healer, Keremet-apke. Keremet-apke felt Yerzhan's pulse, kneaded the bones in his fingers and led him behind a curtain. She tore the curtain material in half, sat next to the boy and appealed to Tengri, and to the prophet Makhambet, and to Makhambet's angel. She swayed from side to side, working herself up more and more, then grabbed a whip and lashed herself across the knees and lashed the boy gently across his shoulders and back. 'The devil's work! The devil's work!' Foam poured out of her babbling mouth and she gestured to her daughter, who stood by the door: 'Bring it!' And in an instant her daughter had fetched a scorching-hot sheep's shoulder blade. Keremet-apke cooled it with her saliva and then held it against the boy's back.

Yerzhan was very quickly cured of his infernal fever. But he didn't grow a single finger's breadth.

He hated his granny for believing in all this antediluvian quackery, and most of all for that story of hers about little snot-nosed Gesar that she had told him back in his child-hood. He hated her for the way she gossiped about him with Granny Sholpan for days at a time now, pondering over this life and wondering why he had been left a midget…

Aisulu's father, Shaken, also became angry at the whispering of the two old women and one day in early winter he took Yerzhan to the city for an X-ray. The train travelled through the steppe and they passed the dead city that Uncle Shaken had showed Yerzhan a long time ago. And they passed the Dead Lake. But everything was covered under a fine layer of snow that shifted ceaselessly in the piercing steppe wind, until it gathered in drifts at the railway's snow barriers.

They reached the city – a welter of people, cars and houses – and travelled through this dizzying, cramped space to a special clinic, where they led Yerzhan into a room and told him to undress and stand between the metal parts of a large device which Uncle Shaken called an X-ray machine. They switched off the light and made clicking noises.

Afterwards, Uncle Shaken and Yerzhan waited in the corridor until a man in a white coat and cap came out and showed Shaken black pages with bright spots on them.

'Perfectly normal bones,' the man said. 'The bones of a child. Only there are no growth zones left…'

From the way that Uncle Shaken first argued with the man, then swore, then shouted at everyone, mentioning America and the Soviet Union all in one go, Yerzhan realized that nobody here would help him either. And he quietly hated these men in their doctor's coats, and Uncle Shaken too, with his eternal pursuit of America.

*

Grandad Daulet, too, took his turn at trying to stretch his grandson's bones. His method was an old folk one. Without telling the grannies or the younger generation, he took Yerzhan out into the steppe. There he wrapped him in a tarpaulin railway cloak, tied his hands carefully with a lasso, put a felt shawl under him, tied the other end of the lasso to his own waist and mounted his horse. He moved off at a trot that became faster and faster until it turned into a gallop across the sandy soil, dragging his grandson behind him, lying stretched out on the ground. Yerzhan's eyes and mouth filled up with fine sand that still grated on his teeth in the evening and could only be extracted from his nose by sneezing. And his arms ached from the knots of the lasso. But even this procedure didn't add any height to him.

At night Grandad shouted at Granny Ulbarsyn for everyone to hear because she had produced a good-for-nothing daughter, while the daughter, Yerzhan's mother, sat in silence in the next room, crying over her son. As Yerzhan fell asleep, gazing up drowsily at his poor, dumb mother, he quietly hated Grandad for his swearing, and for the pointless daily torment, and for the sand that had crept into his crotch and in under his tailbone, and for the salt on his lips.

Even Kepek, who had become Yerzhan's bitterest enemy ever since he saw his uncle riding on the donkey with Aisulu, tried to help his nephew. He lent Yerzhan the only iron bedstead in the house for a few nights. He tied Yerzhan's hands to the head frame, tied his feet to the opposite end and left him there, crucified for the night. The boy dreamt that he was flying over the steppe like Gesar on his steed, and the feather grass was swept aside under the hooves, and the sky opened up to meet him. And instead of the sun, Aisulu's face greeted him.

Yerzhan had abandoned his violin. But that winter he played on his *dombra* almost all night and day. During the day, when Grandad went to knock the snow off his points and rails, when Kepek took Aisulu to school and the women spun wool, Yerzhan was left alone, and he took the *dombra* and played the same song over and over again: '*Aidan aru narsa zhok*' – 'Nothing is there purer than the moon'. He played it to a thousand different melodies.

> *Nothing is there purer than the moon,*
> *But it abides by night, and not by day.*
> *Nothing is there purer than the sun,*
> *But it abides by day and not by night.*
> *True Islam abides not in anyone –*
> *They have it on their tongues, not in their hearts.*

To Yerzhan this old song was about him. Every word of it, every sentence that followed another, was telling the story of his life. How sweetly it had all begun, as if the entire world consisted of the pure moon and the pure sun, of his Aisulu and him. But didn't the song warn him? And how could he forget: the moon shines only at night and the sun shines only during the day. Only once a year do moon and sun appear together at the two sides of the steppe, like two huge, identical circles. Or had he just seen that in a dream?

Who cared about him? Everyone simply pretended, especially those two old grannies. But the others too: look at his grandad – his only real concern was keeping his points lubricated. Or Uncle Shaken, with his work shifts, during which he tried to catch up with and overtake America. Or Kepek and Aisulu, and the donkey as well! Yerzhan was the only one who didn't belong among them, Yerzhan was the only one who didn't fit into their lives at all…

Fools, fools, fools: one took him to a quack medicine woman, another quartered him alive with horses, and as for the one who was educated – he couldn't do anything either, even with an X-ray and a reactor!

What could Yerzhan do now? He couldn't go to school – all those kids were a head taller than him already. They'd laugh in his face. Stay here with this ignorant crowd, where everyone had suddenly forgotten that he had nibbled Aisulu's ear as his bride-to-be? No, now they would never live together, under the moon or the sun!

He could see it all. And see even more things that he didn't want to put into words. Images built up inside this petrified body and inside his morbid soul, which was ageing against his will. Did any of it do him any good? Did it make him even the slightest bit taller?

Every time Yerzhan saw Aisulu, Kepek and the donkey in the bluish gloom of the steppe's winter twilight – through the frame of a doorway, through a window or from behind the wall where he was hiding – he wanted to grab Grandad's double-barrelled shotgun or Granny's kitchen knife, or even Kepek's own railway hammer, the one he used to hammer on the trains' motionless wheels at night, and dart out to meet them, to shoot, stab and kill all three of them. But each time something in his little body stopped him. What it was, he simply couldn't make out. He suffered torment all night through until the morning, all day through until the evening, but he couldn't find the answer. Like a schoolboy who has lost his exercise book and crib sheet.

And once again his rebellion was put off until the next day. If this was the way of things in the world, then weren't his suffering, his imaginings and threats, all his thoughts, like a flowing stream, like powdered snow, like a swirling blizzard and his life simply a short, sad song?

No, his life wasn't a song. His life resembled more the chain reaction once demonstrated by Uncle Shaken, where all started from his hatred for Grandad, or for Granny, or for Kepek and the donkey, or for Uncle Shaken or… His life was like a chain reaction, and so was everyone else's too. And perhaps even through his petrified boy's body an abrupt adulthood was forcing its way out, as Yerzhan started to see what he hadn't noticed before. Not only did he notice Kepek sitting on the donkey with his arms around Aisulu's body (although that was most painful of all), but he also saw Kepek disappearing from home when Shaken was at work and reappearing at city bride Baichichek's house, moving out Granny Sholpan under various pretexts to her friend Ulbarsyn. Of course, he could simply be fetching salt, or a nail, or be helping to bone meat. But truth to tell, what Kepek got up to over there when Aisulu came running to Yerzhan to tell him what was happening at school and how the boys and girls missed him – no one really dared ask.

Kepek returned from Baichichek's house all flushed and agitated, as if he had chopped an entire cow to pieces, not just helped bone the meat. Then he grabbed his hammer and left, whistling a tune that only he knew, puffing and panting, not wrapped up against the cold, to replace his father on the points or in the siding.

But one day Aisulu herself confessed in secret that her mother took Kepek soup at night. After all, she said, he had chopped the bones, the poor man was probably freezing and he was as good as a brother in their house.

But was Shaken any better than Kepek? One day, when Grandad Daulet and Uncle Kepek were dealing with an express special, and Granny Ulbarsyn had gone to Granny Sholpan to wash her hair with sour milk, Yerzhan heard cautious tapping at the next window – his mother's window – followed by a rustle of footsteps in the next room. At first Yerzhan thought it was a bird fluttering against the windowpane in the cold. In order not to frighten it away with his shadow, the boy looked out cautiously through his window at a narrow angle, hiding in the corner of the room. But it wasn't a bird. It was Uncle Shaken. Why didn't he knock at the door? Yerzhan heard the door of the next room creak and pressed his back hard against the wall, terrified of being caught spying. Thank God, his mother didn't look into his room. She slipped out of the house, throwing on her camel-wool shawl as she went.

Yerzhan stood there with his heart pumping hard, pounding its rhythm against the wall – or was that the heavy passenger express that pounded on the rails with a rhythm that pulsed through the ground? Whatever the cause of the pounding, Yerzhan just stood there nailed to the floor, more dead than alive. And once again that same implacable, visceral fear rose up from his trembling knees to his stomach, where it stopped like a hot, heavy, aching lump.

His mother slipped past his window and there, under her window, where he could only see the sheared-off tops of their figures, they talked about something that Yerzhan, who was all ears now, simply couldn't make out. What they could be talking about out there on the firm, white snow, with wisps of hot steam coming out of their mouths, Yerzhan never found out. And was his dumb mother really speaking, or was it only the steam that Yerzhan took for conversation – who could say? Yerzhan didn't mention this incident to anyone. Not even to his Aisulu, who wasn't his any longer.

And then Granny Ulbarsyn, almost falling asleep while Yerzhan was massaging the rheumatic knots on her old woman's legs, muttered about Grandad – he was to blame for all these bumps on her legs, she said. In her young days, when she had only just come to this 'spot', to this Kara-Shagan, Sholpan's husband, Nurpeis, was summoned to the city for training, and Daulet was left as the only man in charge of both families. That winter Daulet kitted himself out to go to his points, leaving Ulbarsyn strict instructions not to venture out in the cold. 'Listen,' he said, 'that's the jackals howling.' Then he took his double-barrelled shotgun and his railway hammer and went out into the blizzard.

Ulbarsyn sat alone for a long time, but boredom is worse than fear, after all, and she wanted to see her friend Sholpan, so she wrapped herself in her shawl. She walked up to her friend's door, where, in the snowy wind, the metal hinge was rattling against the door – tap-tap-tap! Nevertheless Ulbarsyn knocked, but perhaps Sholpan took it for the tapping of the metal hinge. In any case, no one opened the door. Granny Ulbarsyn walked up to the only bright window and glanced in through the gap between the embroidered net curtains. And saw her husband inside. She gasped out loud in fury, gulping in cold, frosty air, and fainted into a snowdrift.

On the way back from his tracks, Daulet found her frozen to the bone and dragged her home, swearing and weeping at the same time. He swore to her by milk and by bread that he had only dropped in to see Sholpan for a moment, to get Nurpeis's lantern. But even if no scar of distrust was left on Ulbarsyn's soul, that night had remained with her for ever as the rheumatism in her bones and muscles.

Yerzhan could no longer tell what was true in these words and what was made up. He thought of his confusion bursting out in its full glorious fury from his petrified body. He recalled the ancient song that Grandad had sung to Petko, about hollow straws floating in a stream, striking first against a rock and then against a branch leaning down over the water. That was him, a straw broken off short, hollow on the inside, with his whistling soul driven into a thin, fragile little body. Sometimes he would strike against a stone or a blade of grass. And no matter how his soul whistled and tweeted, the stream still carried it on towards that dead backwater, where there was no living grass, only silt. And nothing remained of this journey except the movement of air through a hollow inner space, like a song almost too faint to hear.

Part Three

Sol Mi Fa
The Salt of the Myth

We got carried away by our travellers' tales and in the meantime evening fell. What words can convey that melancholy yearning of evening in the steppe, with a solitary train travelling through it? How can I explain that extraordinarily faint song of the air passing through a straw? I tried to recall the poem 'In the Carriage' – I think it's by Innokentii Annensky – which expresses these feelings more accurately than anything else:

> *Enough of doing and of talking,*
> *Let's drop the smiles and stop the words.*
> *The clouds are low, blank snow is falling*
> *And heaven's light is wan and blurred.*
>
> *Enmeshed in strife beyond their knowing,*
> *Black willows writhe in frantic fits.*
> *I say to you, 'Until tomorrow:*
> *For this day you and I are quits.'*
>
> *Setting aside dreaming and pleading –*
> *Though I am boundlessly to blame –*

I wish to gaze at snow-white fields
Through this white-felted windowpane.

Stand tall and be a man,
Assure me you have forgiven,
Join the light of the setting sun,
Around which everything has frozen.

But the stripes of the sunset, around which everything had frozen, quickly faded away and we were left in darkness, deliberately not switching on the light in the compartment. Yerzhan went out to smoke in the corridor and the old man who occupied the bottom bunk opposite me went off for a wash at the other end of the carriage. He returned, muttering a few words, and immediately stretched out once more, turning his face away to the wall.

Yerzhan finished his smoke and came back in again, but he didn't want to talk, or so it seemed to me. I was still in a strange lethargic state after the steppe sunset and the poem retrieved from my subconscious.

I went out into the corridor too and stood there for a while, looking at the solid darkness of the open expanse. Then I hastily washed in the toilet and went back to the compartment, to find both of my travelling companions snoring.

I made up my own bed and lay down, but sleep simply wouldn't come.

*

The daytime steppe, with its endless poles and wires, rose up before me in a vision of infinite musical staves with bars and notes. I tried to read the music, to understand the meaning. But I couldn't. Then I imagined how this story might end, keeping the corner of my eye on the upper bunk, where the twenty-seven-year-old boy lay curled up in a tight ball. Well, he hadn't lied to me, had he? I'd seen his passport, and in the final analysis, even if he was a wunderkind, he couldn't be a wunderkind in everything – playing the violin like a god, and telling the story of his life like a traditional steppe bard, and deceiving me, like an experienced card sharp or an actor. It was too much to fit in one diminutive body; it couldn't all be a confidence trick.

So what had taken place in the time between *it* happening and the present day – or rather, night – in which I simply couldn't get to sleep?

Like our train following its tracks across the steppe, I tried to trace out the line from what I had heard to what I didn't know.

Aisulu grew taller and taller. She was already almost the same height as Kepek. And yet she didn't seem to notice that Yerzhan had stopped growing, that he barely reached up to her shoulder. After school she ran to tell him about her progress, about how today she had played a piece on the violin that Yerzhan used to play three years ago. And the way she ignored what was happening to

Yerzhan infuriated him most of all. He didn't listen to her, he just lay there, staring fixedly at the white ceiling. He didn't get up off Kepek's bed, in order not to look ludicrously small beside her – and she didn't notice. Or she pretended not to.

How could Yerzhan know that she cried at night too, tucked up in bed with her head under the sheets, that she was dreaming of qualifying as a doctor and finding a cure that would stretch out her Yerzhan.

Yerzhan rarely slept at night now, and it wasn't as if he caught up during the day – no, sleep simply wouldn't come to his eyes. He tossed and turned from one side to the other, caught in the same circle of burdensome thoughts that were impossible either to control or to accept. A strange, indeterminate music that had lost its bearings between the *dombra* and the violin was sawing away inside him.

> *The bold Gesar did not enjoy his happiness and peace for long. A terrible demon, the cannibal Lubsan, attacked his country from the north. But Lubsan's wife, Tumen Djergalan, fell in love with Gesar and revealed her husband's secret to him. Gesar used the secret and killed Lubsan. Tumen Djergalan didn't waste any time and gave Gesar a draught of forgetfulness to drink in order to bind him to her for ever. Gesar drank the draught, forgot about*

his beloved Urmai-sulu and stayed with Tumen Djergalan.

Meanwhile, in the steppe kingdom, a rebellion arose and Kara-Choton forced Urmai-sulu to marry him. But Tengri did not desert Gesar and freed him of the enchantment on the very shore of the Dead Lake, where Gesar saw the reflection of his own magical steed. He returned on this steed home to the steppe kingdom and killed Kara-Choton, freeing his Urmai-sulu…

Yerzhan had never forgotten this ancient tale. He of course knew who the Kara-Choton in his life was – Kepek. So at night he tried to guess who resembled the terrible demon Lubsan. Grandad Daulet? But his wife was Granny Ulbarsyn. She couldn't possibly be in love with Yerzhan. And Petko didn't fit either, because he didn't have any wife at all. Uncle Shaken? Could Baichichek be Tumen Djergalan? And then would he have to kill Shaken? The pieces didn't fit. But Yerzhan was convinced that this story, like those ancient songs he played out in his head, was about him. He had to solve the mystery that had sunk its claws into his body and soul.

'The Zone! The Zone! That's the terrible demon Lubsan.' He suddenly sat up straight in bed. The Zone had taken him captive, the Zone had given him the draught of forgetfulness to drink, and until he reached the Dead Lake – the same Dead Lake in which he had once bathed – he would never be freed from this enchantment. Didn't the story say that there, by the Dead Lake, Tengri would free him of the enchantment and show him his own reflection and the reflection of the magical steed on which he had galloped throughout his childhood?

Yerzhan made up his mind.

Day after day that late autumn when Aisulu rode to school alone, when Grandad was sleeping after his night shift and Kepek had gone off to replace either Shaken, away from home because of his work, at Baichichek's house, or his father, Daulet, in the siding, when the old women were warming their bones in front of the house in the last sun, Yerzhan mounted the horse and galloped across the steppe towards the gullies and pastureland where the Zone began. He knew the way. How often had he come this way as a boy with Kepek or Shaken? He followed the dried-up riverbed until he reached the open space of the Zone.

Yerzhan entered the Zone gradually, bit by bit. After all, the fear, that lay in waiting at his hamstrings and could rise up at any moment through the heavy weight in his stomach to his throat, was invincible, it pulsed in his blood, in his very breath. But day after day his determination led him on ever further.

That year the autumn was long and sunny. Yerzhan galloped on and on beyond the Dead City that he had once visited with Uncle Shaken, on along the dry, red riverbed. He discovered gigantic craters of churned-up steppe, as if the moon had decided to observe her own reflection, like him, in order to free herself of an enchantment. He saw strange structures jutting out of the fused earth like limbs of uncanny beings. And still deeper inside the Zone, a concrete wall stood in the middle of the wide expanse, a charred elm tree and black birds imprinted on it. Were they drawings? Or a real tree and real birds stamped into the wall? Yerzhan didn't stop. He galloped on further and further across this hell on earth.

Returning home in the evening, the boy sneaked to his room and lay on his bed without touching either the long-forgotten *dombra* or the violin gathering dust in a niche in the wall. Here, amid the constant chatter of the old women and the rumbling noises of passing trains, the distant radio and television sounds, he suddenly became aware how quiet the Zone was. So quiet that it set his ears ringing.

Like his mother's eternal silence.

Perhaps his unspeaking mother, Kanyshat, held the key to the mystery that controlled his life and body. Perhaps he shouldn't search for any Dead Lake. Perhaps he should free his mother from her enchantment? Perhaps if words could leave her mouth, then the spell would fall away from his puny body? And the steed of his childhood would gallop once again to rescue his Aisulu.

But his mother didn't speak. She walked into the room like a shadow and brought him his supper and collected his laundry for washing. And sometimes at night she stood by her sleeping son's bedside, choking on silent tears.

Yerzhan soon realized that he couldn't reach the Dead Lake within a day's horse ride. It was too far away. But nonetheless something stronger than fear and keener than hope drew him back, day after day, along that dried-up river, into the Zone, which became ever more familiar, ever more like home. An enchantment had indeed seized his entire being, a forgetfulness. Not only had he forgotten the *dombra* and the violin, not only Grandad, Petko and Dean Reed, but even Aisulu: the way she grew ever taller, the way she came back from school, what she said and how she laughed. The road to the Dead Lake along the bed of the dried-up river, the road to the very heart of this mute Zone, now beat to the monotonous, naked rhythm of his galloping steed, and his pounding heart, and his pulsing temple. And there was no space in this rhythm for any music.

Early in the morning of 22 November, as soon as Grandad returned from the night round of the tracks, without bothering to wait for sleepy Kepek or cheerful Aisulu to appear, Yerzhan slipped out of the house and jumped onto the horse that was still warm from carrying the old man. Perhaps because of the abrupt change from a heavy rider to the light body of a boy, or perhaps because of the early-morning hour, Aigyr galloped lightly, as if the wind was not flying in his face but pushed him on from behind. Yerzhan was so intoxicated by the speed, the flight, that he was already inside the Zone before he suddenly discovered his Grandad's double-barrelled shotgun, forgotten between the saddle girth and the stirrup strap. But it was too late to go back. The boy galloped on into the Zone like a genuine spirit, feeling the metal of the barrel with his calves.

He remembered the fox hunt. The thought occurred to him that *it* had happened because they had taken away the fox's little cub. For an instant he felt as if the horse was slipping out from under him. He forced himself to stay in the saddle, as '*kaltarys!*' – the word that indicated a ninety-degree turn – came crashing into his awareness. Yes, his entire life had been *kaltarys* after *kaltarys*, until that *uluu kaltarys* had arrived – that large, great turning – and now he was sprawled out like a carcass yet to be shot, hemmed in on all sides.

His feverish thoughts kept time with the galloping horse. He soon realized that even the non-existent, dried-up river swung from side to side, following those same *kaltarys*. Its course ran from the ground of its conception all the way to the Dead Town, then turned abruptly and ran on until it reached the lunar craters. There it took another oblique turn and ran on again until it reached that crooked concrete wall with the scorched steppe elm and imprinted birds. In his ardent excitement Yerzhan was now certain that the next turn would mean his final turn, and he galloped faster and faster, lashing Aigyr on with the whip...

*

And as the sun fell behind in its pursuit of him, he suddenly spotted a small outcrop in the middle of the open steppe. A solitary dog or fox or wolf. The galloping horse drew closer. A wolf. Yerzhan didn't slow Aigyr. He pulled out Grandad's shotgun from under the saddle girth at full speed and, without bothering to aim, just to frighten the creature, fired into the air with one barrel. The wolf flew off in the same direction as Aigyr and Yerzhan. And once again Yerzhan found himself in pursuit of a wolf, like so many years ago with Aisulu on the donkey. He whooped at the top of his lungs and the wolf ran without a backward glance. Because of the shot, fervent Aigyr strove even harder, forcing on the incessant movement of his hooves.

Then all of a sudden the wolf disappeared into the ground.

What was it? A mirage that had sprung from the boy's overheated and inflamed imagination? Salt, glittering in the bright autumn sun? A stretch of stagnant water, lying here since the summer? The shore of the Dead Lake? Yerzhan arrived at the spot where the wolf had disappeared. Right in front of him was a cliff. Reining in Aigyr, he stopped where the slope down to the shore was shallow. He didn't let the horse approach the water, even though it must have been thirsty after the non-stop run. Instead he tied the reins firmly, with a double knot, to a fused metal rail sticking up out of the earth. He walked to the water, the shotgun loaded with its second cartridge firmly in his hand. No sight of the wolf. It had disappeared, as if drowned.

The water was dark blue, its own blueness added to the blueness of the sky. Yerzhan saw his reflection as a vague blob. His eyes had grown tired from the uninterrupted galloping, with nothing but the yellow steppe flowing into them. At first he wanted to drink his fill of the thick water, but then he decided not to waste time. Without getting undressed, he slid into the lake awkwardly off the bank, fully clothed, with the shotgun in his hands, feet first. The coolness seared his body, and just as he expected to sink completely underwater, a strange force suddenly pushed him out and he found himself lying on his back on the surface, like a boat. What kind of force was this? It surely wasn't the shotgun that was keeping him afloat! Yerzhan had read that in the Dead Sea, between Jordan and Palestine, it was impossible to drown, because the water was so salty. He tried tasting the water, but his parched tongue couldn't identify the taste of salt. So he lay there, unable to comprehend if this experience was real or a dream. And slowly his swaying body began to melt. And it began to stretch. Longer and longer: the same way the bow of his violin tensed up before he played, the same way the strings stretched out when he tuned them. And now the bow would touch the strings and the music would sound.

'A long, long time ago there was a boy called Wolfgang. Do you know what that name means? Walking wolf.' Yerzhan shuddered at that – perhaps it was cunning Petko who had sent the wolf into the steppe? 'This

> *boy was such a talented musician that he could play*
> *any instrument with his eyes blindfolded...'*

Yerzhan's soul felt as light as air, as if his little body had dissolved in this bitter water. He wanted so badly to preserve the feeling, to prevent himself from spilling it, that there was nothing left of him but waiting and listening.

Yerzhan galloped back across the steppe on the horse, and the sun at his back stretched out his shadow, longer and longer, as if the enchantment had fallen away from him and now he would return to the world where slim, stately Aisulu was waiting for him. He galloped across the steppe on the horse, with the gun in his hand, feeling like Dean Reed again in one of his films about Indians, when he played the cowboy Joe. And now he sang out as loud as he could, at the top of his lungs, for the whole steppe to hear, for the whole sky to hear:

> *My love is tall, as tall as mountains,*
> *My love is deep, as deep as a sea...*

On the very point of sunset, when his shadow was flattened so far out across the steppe that he couldn't see where it ended, the low sun behind him lit up the hills where he was conceived. And in the sunset glow he saw two horses, tied to a tamarisk bush. Yerzhan's heart started pounding rapidly and his horse, sensing danger, switched to a stealthy trot. As he approached the place of his conception, Dean Reed's song faded from his lips and his lungs, and that phrase, *uluu kaltarys*, returned, throbbing in time with his heart, his pulse, his breathing.

And suddenly he saw what he had been afraid of seeing all his life. Down below among the sand and stones of the dried-up riverbed Aisulu lay stretched out, with Kara-Choton – the loathsome Kepek – leaning down towards her over and over again. Yerzhan reined in the horse and dismounted and grabbed Grandad's shotgun with both hands. He didn't tether Aigyr, merely waved his hand and hissed. The obedient horse stood still. Running from bush to bush like in a cowboy film, Yerzhan crept to within calling distance.

He took aim and fired the remaining cartridge.

The fear that had lurked within him all his life suddenly stirred, brushing past his stomach, flying up to his throat and bursting out in a frenetic, childish scream. Kepek collapsed onto Aisulu like a limp sack. Yerzhan dashed forward, watching with utter horror as a strip of gauze, as bright red with his uncle's blood as a streak of sunset, fell out of Kepek's hands on to Aisulu's white leg, which was left only half-bandaged.

Aisulu had broken her leg looking for Yerzhan.

No, I didn't even try to think this story through to the end; it was too terrible for this quiet steppe night with the gentle hammering of the train's wheels and my heart beating in time with them. The boy on the upper bunk was muttering incomprehensible words in his sleep, the old man opposite me was snoring nervously, like a ram that has just been stuck. What a nightmare! I thought. Blaming my fears on the stale air in the compartment, I stood up and opened the door slightly. A cool draught was blowing from the corridor. I decided to wait a while for the compartment to cool completely, so I didn't lie down again.

The train ran on tirelessly across the night-time steppe. A rare light, or perhaps a star that had fought its way through the dense darkness, moved slowly round the train. When the compartment had filled up with the chilly night air, I cautiously closed the door, but as if responding to my movement, the train slowed and suddenly, with the usual screech of brake blocks in the night, it stopped. I listened. In the distance steps rustled sporadically across the gravel of the embankment. Whoever it was kept stopping, and then the steps would start again, moving closer and getting clearer. Finally, somewhere underneath us, a lantern glinted for a moment, a hammer clanged against brake blocks and a trembling voice spoke into the darkness in Kazakh: 'So that's it! Fuck it…'

I suddenly wanted to shake Yerzhan awake, but I managed to stop myself.

Yerzhan was sleeping uneasily, as usual. They had only just buried Granny Ulbarsyn and the old women from the entire district, led by Keremet-apke, the local healer, were still performing their shamanic rituals and saying their prayers at Granny Sholpan's house. Having lost his wife, Grandad had borne up manfully all the way through the funeral, but on the third day he had gone limp and taken to his bed. Shaken was left to chop wood alone for the hearth under the immense cauldron, go running to the tracks and back, and slaughter a sheep for the wake.

The way Granny Ulbarsyn had died was strange. In late autumn the lumps on her legs had started swelling up, and no matter how hard Yerzhan rubbed them, they kept getting bigger. 'Ah, my lumps grow bigger but you haven't. And you haven't got any stronger either,' Granny Ulbarsyn moaned in undisguised reproach.

The city bride Baichichek had tried to persuade her husband, Shaken, to take old Granny Ulbarsyn to the city for an X-ray, but the old woman flatly refused. Instead she persuaded her own husband to take her on a camel to the healer Keremet-apke. Keremet-apke felt Granny's pulse, kneaded the bones in her fingers and led her behind a curtain. She tore the material of the curtain in half and then sat beside Granny Ulbarsyn and appealed to Tengri, and to the prophet Makhambet, and to the prophet's angel. She swayed from side to side, working herself up more and more, then grabbed a whip off the wall and first lashed herself across the knees with it, then lashed the old woman's legs gently. 'The devil's work! The devil's work!' And when foam started pouring out of her babbling mouth, she gestured to her daughter standing by the door: 'Bring it!' And in an instant her daughter had fetched a scorching-hot sheep's shoulder blade. Keremet-apke cooled it with her saliva and then held it against Granny Ulbarsyn's legs.

'For nine days plus nine feed a black ram with twisted horns and then slaughter it on Tuesday!' she ordered. 'Rub the warm blood on your legs and you'll skip and hop like a two-year-old gazelle!'

But alas, there wasn't a black ram with twisted horns in the flock, and on the next market day Grandad galloped off to the cattle yard at the regional centre and brought one back on a lead – not just a ram, but a real devil with horns. The devil kicked out and butted and refused to be held. Grandad and Shaken could barely contain him, and to prevent him from butting the whole flock to death, they had to tie him by the neck and knot his legs.

Although Grandad brought the ram on Sunday, Granny Ulbarsyn calculated that she should only start feeding him on Friday, so that nine days plus nine would fall on a Tuesday. The next Friday she got up out of the bed she had lain in almost all autumn and tottered off, taking small steps, first to the hay and then to the pen, where that devil was tethered, and threw an armful of hay down in front of him. She did this twice a day, and with every day her legs grew stronger and her stride became ever more sure.

The ram grew fatter and fatter, Granny felt better and better and the lumps on her legs shrank day by day. The night before the appointed Tuesday, after feeding the devil that had now become a friend and with whom she had long conversations, Granny came back cheerfully to the house and asked Grandad for advice.

'Daulet, what do you think? Should we really slaughter that ram tomorrow?'

'Why do you ask?' Grandad asked in surprise.

'Well, I just thought, my legs are working well now, and I've got used to having the ram around…'

'Go to bed,' said Grandad. 'I've got to go out for the 5.27!'

The next day, despite Granny's peevish opposition, they decided to slaughter the ram. We'll rub the warm blood on your legs, and on Yerzhan's legs too, they said. Who knows, perhaps someone put a spell on the ram. It might do some good. Shaken and Grandad went to tie up the ram, and Granny sat down by the door, preparing her legs for the fresh blood. Yerzhan sat a little distance away and observed the goings-on, more out of idle curiosity than any hope of being cured.

And then, when Shaken took the rope off the ram's neck and grasped him, ready to throw him over on his side, the devil, grown strong from all his fine feeding, suddenly kicked out with a grunt, knocked Grandad over with a single movement, darted out of the pen and dashed towards Granny as fast as he could. He flew towards her like a terrified child flying to its mother's embrace, like a tame eagle flying to the hunter's arm, like a she-fox's cub flying to its den.

The fattened black devil with twisted horns crashed into the old woman at full tilt.

And that's how Granny Ulbarsyn met her death.

They slaughtered the ram that very day – not, as had been expected, to cure old Granny Ulbarsyn, but for her funeral.

In all the fuss and commotion over Granny Ulbarsyn's sudden death, of course they forgot to rub the warm blood on Yerzhan's legs, so he remained under the spell. Well, never mind him, he was used to it already, but Grandad, who plunged his arms up to the elbows into the blood of that devil ram with twisted horns, took to his bed on the third day after his wife's death. 'I'm worn out!' he told Shaken and Yerzhan in a meek little voice. So Shaken started taking Yerzhan with him to the railway tracks to check the points or, when their official railway phone rang, to switch them for a train that was waiting.

No, Grandad didn't die that time. He got up after nine days plus nine, hale and hearty, and went to the old woman's grave by foot to say a prayer.

The next to die was Granny Sholpan. It was in early spring. Perhaps the long winter, spent indoors, had already bored her to death, or she had pined away for her old friend Ulbarsyn. Anyway, when the snow melted and the green land began drying out, Granny Sholpan started taking long walks along the railway line in both directions. Aisulu accompanied her as often as possible and picked poppies to weave a wreath for herself, or dug up snowdrops and carried them home in her hands, like whitish-yellow candles protruding from soft clay lumps.

The day Granny Sholpan died, Aisulu was at school, Shaken was on his shift, Baichichek and Kanyshat were washing the laundry that had accumulated over the winter, Grandad was sleeping after switching a heavy goods train into the siding, where it had been standing motionless for more than two hours, and Yerzhan was sitting by the official phone, waiting for the express passenger train to pass at last and for Grandad to be told to switch the points to dispatch the goods train. On that sunny morning old Sholpan went for her walk alone. Poppies beat against her legs, but she walked on, in a black jacket and wide green dress, as tall and stately as a poplar tree, with her hands clasped behind her back. 'That's who Aisulu takes after!' Yerzhan thought bitterly as he watched Granny Sholpan's figure disappear.

And what happened next was this: the black cock, who had been ruffling the chickens' feathers in the morning, assumed that Granny Sholpan had come out to feed him and ran after her. The unsuspecting old woman was walking along the railway line, when suddenly she saw a piece of bread roll lying by her feet. An unbeliever must have thrown it out of the window of a train – the locals wouldn't throw bread away. Granny Sholpan bent down, picked up the bread and kissed it three times, then threw it under the stationary goods train, onto the railway embankment, thinking to herself that the train would leave and a bird would peck it up. But the cock, seeing the bread, rushed towards it. The old woman was taken by surprise. She never let her birds go near the railway; she always kept them in the yard behind the house. And now she was frightened that the chickens would follow the cock. So she glanced round at the stationary train, bent over and ducked under it. The cock was so absorbed in his pecking that he only shook his head from side to side and took no notice of her. 'You're sitting there like a broody hen with a chick under her wing. Better you should die!' Granny Sholpan squawked, climbing out from under the wagon onto the embankment. Eventually, she managed to shoo off the cock all right, but just then, whistling and hooting like a blast from the Zone, the passenger express came flying up on the next line. And although there was enough space between the two trains – the one standing still and the one flying past – Granny Sholpan's wide green satin dress billowed up in the swirling air and a footplate caught its hem.

The poor old woman was dragged along the embankment until the satin shredded into bloodstained tatters.

Strangely enough, only after the two old women were gone was Yerzhan able to tell the other members of the households apart. Until then they had formed one entity: if Granny Sholpan scolded him, then Granny Ulbarsyn slapped him. If his mother, Kanyshat, kneaded the dough, then city bride Baichichek moulded the bread rolls. But suddenly the solid units dissolved. As soon as Granny Sholpan was buried in the newly extended tomb – beside her husband, Nurpeis, and her old friend Ulbarsyn – city bride Baichichek began to persuade her husband, Shaken, to move to the city. After all, it had been his mother who kept him here, Baichichek argued. But now she was gone, so why should they waste their lives at this godforsaken way station? Shaken kept avoiding the conversation with promises that when he came home from his next shift, then they would sit down and talk things over. Or they should mark the anniversary of his mother's death first and then decide. But according to Aisulu, Baichichek insisted more and more. And that was when Yerzhan realized that these two families had been united by the two old women, Ulbarsyn and Sholpan. And anyway, his mother had stopped going to Baichichek's house altogether now, hadn't she!

Yerzhan looked at his mother. She had always been a kind of ever-present absence for him. He had been raised by the entire 'spot', and above all by Grandad and the two grannies. Now that the two women were dead, Grandad had stopped swaggering and putting on airs, and a more distinct image of his mother arose in Yerzhan's heart.

His mother never stopped working for a moment. She might be trimming the hair off a goatskin, then sprinkling it with warm water, rolling it up into a tube and setting it close to the stove. Then, while the skin was warming to release the hair roots more easily, she'd start spinning string out of the hair that she had just trimmed off. After finishing that job, she would knead dough. After wrapping the dough to help it rise, she would bring in the fresh milk, pour some into crocks to produce cream, and mix the rest with sour milk, so that by morning the mixture would have turned sour too. Then she would open the rolled-up goat skin and scrape it, and then, after drying it over the flames, immerse it in sour milk and leave it to soak for a few days. Towards evening she would darn torn clothes, boil up soup and make her bed. In short, she never stopped working from morning till night.

And if Yerzhan's way of wasting away his life was to do nothing at all, his mother, Kanyshat, on the contrary, seemed to be scouring the life out of her body with incessant work.

One early summer's day Yerzhan picked up his violin again. There was no one at home. And perhaps it was the thought of his mother, or the possible misery of Shaken's family leaving, but most likely it was his longing for Aisulu that drove him back into the arms of music. He poured the immense grief that had been compressed in his puny body for so long into the instrument. But the grieving didn't end and the music couldn't hold all his accumulated feelings. When Shaken returned from his shift and found Yerzhan still playing, he remarked joyfully that Petko was back, he'd seen him in the city. Yerzhan decided that he would mount the horse to see his teacher the next day. But the next day his grandad galloped away on the horse about his own business, leaving Yerzhan to mind the phone. And the day after that Shaken galloped off on the horse to the school, to enquire about Aisulu's examinations. After a few days Yerzhan was tired of waiting for Aigyr, so he mounted the donkey and trudged off in the direction of the Mobile Construction Unit. The violin was slung on his back like a rifle, and even though his shadow in front became shorter and shorter, for a moment or two he felt like a cowboy again.

> *While the men keep on dying*
> *And the women keep on crying,*
> *The war goes on and on...*

The song kept him going. After about an hour, he reached a concrete structure that resembled a goose sticking up in the steppe like a stone sculpture. Yerzhan stopped for a break in its shade. But before he could dismount, the sky above him, all of a sudden and without any forewarning, turned dark. The bright sunlight flooding the steppe must have exhausted my eyes, he thought. He blinked and the sky turned pitch black, leaving only the sun as a glittering bright circle. And the fear started moving once again from his ankles upwards to root itself in his stomach. Yerzhan was all alone in the immense, wide world – if you didn't count his frenziedly wailing donkey. But not for long and soon even the wailing of the donkey was lost in the roaring and howling of the wind. The ground shook and thunder roared. Burning clumps of tumbleweed swept across the steppe. And a second sun soared up into the sky. Yerzhan, guided not by reason but by instinct, flung himself into a pit that his donkey had already collapsed into, right in under the concrete. The violin crunched and gave a final squeal, and a ferocious, swirling vortex of air hurtled past, whooping deafeningly as it shaved off everything above them, making way for a grey, dusty light to rise over the world.

Then a hot drizzle fell.

Yerzhan lay sprawled in the pit, mingled with the mud, blood and tears. His donkey had instantly gone bald.

He did reach the Mobile Construction Unit eventually. Or what was left of it. Two shattered and melted tractors and the black ashes of the trailers scattered across the steppe.

He could hear a solitary wolf howling somewhere as it died, leaving no trace.

Upon his return to the way station, he immediately noticed that Kapty's fur had come off and everywhere – from the railway tracks as far as the house – the grass had grown thick and tall in just a day… He alone hadn't grown…

I didn't continue with this idea. Outside the carriage window the night was so black that I suddenly experienced a fear which I thought must be similar to that of Yerzhan, who was now slumbering peacefully on the upper bunk of our compartment. Where this fear came from, I did not know, but the feeling of something inevitable yet hidden, that could be here, just round the next bend, had lodged in my belly as a chilly knot. I couldn't think of anything better to do than turn over on my stomach and bury my face in the skimpy railway pillow. I tried to force myself to think about something bright and cheerful.

Yerzhan had aged in his mind at a stroke. He now looked at beautiful Aisulu, who had grown a head taller than her father, without any bitterness, simply in admiration. The fact that she acted as if nothing had happened to him or to her no longer offended him. Truth to tell, he was glad. After all, she could have despised him. Fate plays mean tricks on everyone, he thought. People live out their lives at different speeds. Take Grandad Daulet: after reaching the age of almost eighty, he lost everything he had – his wife, his daughter, his grandson, his friend and now his friend's family too. Or Yerzhan's mother, Kanyshat: she'd lost everything she had too – her virginity, the chance of a husband, her happiness, her father, her brother, her mother and her son… Why should he, Yerzhan, be any different from them? However, because he was so talented, it had all happened to him much faster. Maybe in a single *mushel* – twelve short years – he had already lived out the life granted to him. After all, he had already lived through everything that is given to a man – the warmth of family, the happiness of love, the infatuation of hopes, the bitterness of disappointments, the music of the soul and the fear of oblivion. And now, like his grandad and his mother, he had lost everything. Perhaps the entire meaning of life was only this and nothing more. Lived out, worn out, exhausted.

Why had all this happened to him? How had he deserved it? By being too talented? Had Petko persuaded his mysterious Wolfgang to lead Yerzhan's soul off along his wolfish paths, leaving him only a child's body for ever? Or had the mother fox, humiliated and insulted in the midst of her native steppe then robbed of her little child, put a curse on him in revenge? Or was it merely a variation, an echo, of what had happened to his own humiliated and insulted mother in the midst of her own steppe? Had his grandad's *dombra* and its ancient songs put a spell on the boy, making him turn *kaltarys* after *kaltarys*, until that final great turning had reversed time, making it run backwards, in defiance of nature? Or had the chain reaction Shaken was using to catch up with and overtake America in this godforsaken steppe, in this hell on earth that was called the Zone, taken place by mistake not in a reactor but in a boy, exploding like a dwarf star inside him? Or had the old grannies enchanted him with that snotty-nosed scamp Gesar, always waging war against his uncle Kepek-Choton, or against the whole world, or against himself?

And then the bright face of his Aisulu, grown extravagantly tall now, would suddenly appear from behind the wild grass that had shot up in a flash, frightening Yerzhan with an obscure association, like a discordant note or the scraping of stone on glass.

*

At that time of early, early morning when the steppe is as grey and cool as the sky that has only just begun to brighten, Yerzhan was woken by the stealthy tapping of a stone at a window. At once he sat up, fully conscious. Someone was knocking, with a slight scrape, at the next window. It was his mother's. For these last few days Yerzhan had slept with his clothes on. He simply tumbled into bed when his thoughts could no longer bear their own incessant weight and slid off into sleep. He glanced out at an angle through his window. It was Shaken, who must have just arrived back from his shift, having hitched a ride on a train that was heading his way. He was carrying his invariable briefcase and something else. He hadn't been home yet. Yerzhan gazed impassively at what was happening. He couldn't see his mother – she was on the other side of the wall – but from the lively way that Shaken was gesticulating, he could guess what this sly interaction was about. After all, it wasn't the first time he had caught Shaken in these intimate exchanges.

Perhaps it was because of the early morning hour, or perhaps for some other reason, but it wasn't anger or jealousy, merely an idle, abstract curiosity that made Yerzhan swing his window open abruptly and stick his head out. Uncle Shaken was taken aback and he dropped his briefcase, but then he got a grip on himself and, as if he had knocked at Kanyshat's window by mistake and was really looking for Yerzhan, he flapped his hand at the other window and turned towards Yerzhan. 'Look what I've brought for you…' he began, then stepped back again towards Kanyshat's window, waved his hand to her, as if to say, 'Don't worry, it was a mistake' – and then opened his little suitcase, rummaged in it and pulled out a newspaper. He unfolded it, stuck one of the pages in through the window and said, 'Read that!'

Yerzhan started reading out loud:

'In June sad news reached us from the GDR. The well-known American singer and actor Dean Reed was killed in an accident. As often happens in such cases, this news gave rise to various kinds of insinuations in the West. Right-wing newspapers made play with the provocative theory that the American singer's death was supposedly connected with "the terrorist activities of the special services of the communist regime of the GDR".

'We phoned the American singer's widow, Renate Blum, in Berlin. Renate told us this: "Any suggestions that my husband was murdered are absolutely outrageous slander. Such speculations only insult Dean's memory and cause pain to me and our daughter. My husband drowned. He was found dead in a lake. Just recently Dean's health had deteriorated badly: he suffered from heart problems. As for the supposition that he wanted to go back to the USA, that too is an absolute lie. He was not intending to do anything of the kind. All his thoughts and energies were focused on a new film. He loved our daughter very much. I consider it squalid chicanery to speculate on the death of my husband

and hope very much that you will convey my precise words."'

The world turned dark in front of Yerzhan's eyes.

Dean Reed too had now been taken away from him. Why did Shaken bring this newspaper from the city? Why had he brought the television? On that television Dean Reed – his Dean Reed, Yerzhan's Dean Reed – was once called 'the Red Elvis'. Yerzhan had never heard of Elvis, and later they had shown Elvis himself, and it appeared that Dean Reed was a kind of fake, not the real thing. And now Shaken had taken away even this fake, counterfeit Dean Reed. Just as he had taken away Yerzhan's height and his future, and his love, and his mother.

For a moment Shaken hesitated, then he set off towards his own house with his little suitcase...

Wait, wait! What if he loved Yerzhan's mother, Kanyshat? And what if he had loved her all his life? Hadn't Yerzhan's grandad told him how he once tied up Shaken when he came back drunk from his shift at night and tried to climb in through Kanyshat's window? It had all been put down to drunkenness at the time, but this wasn't the first time Yerzhan had caught him at his mother's window, was it? And that was why he simply refused to leave and take his city wife, Baichichek, back to the city she longed for.

Stop! That time by the Dead Lake, in the Zone, at Shaken's test site, where he was catching up with and overtaking America, when the kids from the school were running about in gas masks, Shaken was the one who appeared in that Armed Forces Protective Suit – like an alien from another world! And hadn't his granny Ulbarsyn always spoken about an alien when she recalled Yerzhan's miraculous conception on the very outskirts of the Zone, in that very same area where the river with the dried-out bed lay?

Yerzhan dashed into the next room to his mother. She was sitting on the windowsill, maybe with nothing to do for the very first time, with her face half-turned towards the window, following Shaken with her eyes as he moved away. 'Do you love him?' Yerzhan asked, gasping out all his anger and all his confusion. His mother didn't turn towards her son, but merely ran her finger over the glass. 'Does he love you?' Yerzhan blurted out helplessly. His mother unwove the plait on her head, shook her hair out and then wove her plait again, looking at her faint reflection in the windowpane. 'Is he your husband?' Yerzhan asked in a shaky voice, continuing his interrogation. His mother folded her arms across her chest. A thick silence filled the room. The naked light bulb hanging from the ceiling quivered. Immediately the fear lurking in Yerzhan's ankles moved upwards along its usual path to his stomach, paused there as a cold, heavy weight and then slowly crept on up to his throat, and, after choking him for a moment, reached his lips, emerging as something that was neither a whisper, nor a wheeze, nor a convulsion: 'Is he my father?' A faint rumbling ran across the floor, the room started trembling and his mother carried on sitting on the windowsill in the way she had been sitting, doing nothing for the first time in her life, merely gazing out of the window towards yet another train or yet another explosion.

Yerzhan ran out of the room. Run, run, run, out into the open steppe, across the Zone and past the horizon, past the edge of the world… Run from this fear, from this truth, from this life… So his Aisulu, growing extravagantly like the wild grass under the windows, his poor, unhappy Aisulu… and suddenly, like the she-fox after the *uluu kaltarys* – the final, great turn – Yerzhan's consciousness imploded in exhaustion.

Aisulu was dying alone in a ward in the municipal hospital. Her father had brought her here and then had immediately been called to the testing ground. Her mother had stayed with her for the first few days, but had just left to see her aged parents, who lived in Semey. Aisulu lay there alone in the ward with the white ceiling. But she didn't see the white ceiling. She saw the steppe and the road from Kara-Shagan to school and back. There she was, riding on the donkey with her Yerzhan, who had disappeared now, and the donkey suddenly picked up a cabbage stalk that someone had thrown out of a passenger train. The donkey had swallowed it whole and choked and lashed out. And first Aisulu and then Yerzhan tumbled off. Yerzhan shouted at Aisulu and

Aisulu grabbed the reins and Yerzhan put his arm up to the elbow into the donkey's foaming mouth and pulled out the stalk. And then she took the scarf off her head, licked away the blood flowing along Yerzhan's arm and bound the wound tightly.

A stalk, a huge stalk, had now got stuck inside Aisulu's body and her organs were swelling, growing extravagantly, like the rest of her body.

She had admired Yerzhan, the way he played the violin, the way he studied and drew and sang Dean Reed, the way he walked into the Dead Lake, the way he was so protective of her... She had wanted to be his wife, to give him children as talented, brave and devoted as he was, but why had *it* happened to him and not to her? But what was this *it*? Hadn't it happened to her as well? She was lying here, growing extravagantly on the outside and on the inside too, like the wild grass after the blasts, pregnant with her own incurable sickness, all alone in the entire, empty world.

Aisulu looked up again at the ceiling, which was turning bluish just as the last yellow ray of sunlight fell across it like a fox's tail, and the fox cub that had brought her so much joy appeared before her eyes, the one that had crept out of their house unnoticed so many years ago. And Kapty bit it to death. How much weeping and wailing there had been that evening while Kepek buried the fluffy little body, only the size of a kitten. And each night that the mother fox could be heard howling for her dead baby, Kapty howled too, like he did before an atomic explosion.

And now Kapty had started howling in her immense, empty body.

A leaf struck against the hospital window and the sun fell behind the steppe.

A knock at the window woke me from my nightmares to the grey steppe morning. We stood at a way station. An inordinately tall Kazakh woman waved outside the window. She held a little parcel wrapped in newspaper. Yerzhan looked down at her, dangling his short legs. I was so delighted to see him alive and unhurt, as if something irreparable could have happened to him on the line along which the train of my thoughts had been running. But then, hadn't it already happened? What had happened, though? I tried to link what he had told me with the images of my nightmares. I felt as confused as that she-fox out in the open steppe, unable to tell what was truth and what was invention. Where was the inescapable life in all this and where was the inexplicable eternity? Where was what he had lived through and where was what I had invented? Like a train in the steppe, like the consciousness of a Kazakh, like a revolutionary country's impulsive surge into some kind of future, my story only kept hurtling on, further and further. Where was the invisible, virtual wall into which the fox pursued by Kazakh hunters crashes, to collapse in a helpless heap?

There he sat in front of me, a twenty-seven-year-old boy, stuck at the age of twelve, stuck in his twelve-year-old body. What was this all about? Was it time, an entire era of it, that had congealed in him, to be related to me through him, in a single gulp? What was he about, this little man from a big country that no longer existed, that had already lived out its time in an impossible pursuit of America?

What had I discovered for myself through his fate? What unpredictable and crooked experiment had I glanced and seen in him – this wunderkind Yerzhan, imprinted as a crumpled shadow alongside the grass, the trees and the birds in the concrete wall of the Zone, jutting out of the steppe?

And although I knew in my mind that the test site had been closed for a long time already, the same feeling that Yerzhan had repeatedly described to me – that fear lurking in the ankles – rose slowly up through my hollow insides to my stomach, then higher, and higher...

The strapping Kazakh woman knocked on the window and waved her newspaper containing a hot-smoked fish or a piece of bread, or pellets of dried sour milk. Yerzhan leant across, grabbed the two window catches with his strong musician's fingers and opened it, asking, 'What do you want?'

The rasping of the window as it opened and the sound of conversation set the old Kazakh below us stirring and he turned over from one side onto the other – to face us. Yerzhan hung down from his bunk, looking round at the noise, cast a quick glance at the man from his handsomely slanted squirrel's or fox's eyes and suddenly howled out,

'Shaken!' like an eagle screeching at a fox – and flung himself straight at him.

I was seriously frightened. My brain feverishly attempted to complete its line of steppe wires, its music on this stave, its chain reaction, its pursuit of a wolf or a she-fox. He'll strangle him, he'll strangle him, his hands are strong enough to do it – the thought suddenly exploded inside me – and while I was still soaring upwards on the blast wave of this explosion, Yerzhan and the old man were already embracing each other. The old man wept mute tears and the Kazakh woman outside the window froze just as she was, puzzled by what was going on in this carriage, in this compartment, and I didn't understand much of it myself, except that an immense feeling of relief at not having witnessed a quarrel, or a murder, or any other kind of catastrophe, instantly filled me with its eternal, inexpressible, ineffable mystery, like the bright blue sky above the steppe.

An hour later our train halted for a break at an empty way station. Yerzhan and Shaken were still talking to each other in Kazakh, mostly sorrowfully, sighing and mentioning one name over and over again – Aisulu – and from the way they suddenly darted out of the compartment with all their belongings, including a violin slung over a shoulder, I realized that we were standing at Kara-Shagan. I glanced out of the window. Although from the two abandoned Soviet railway houses I could tell that it really was Kara-Shagan, there were no signs of life to be seen – no chickens running around under the single elm some distance away, no old man with a little flag, no hay laid in for the winter, not even a single little cowpat anywhere. Only two figures – one a stooped old man, the other an impetuous boy – moving away past these abandoned, uninhabited houses into the depths of the open plain.

And lit by the sun I could see five graves.

Peirene

Contemporary
World Literature.
Thought provoking,
well designed, short.

*'Two-hour books to be
devoured in a single sitting:
literary cinema for those
fatigued by film.'* TLS

Online Bookshop

Subscriptions

Literary Salons

Reading Guides

Publisher's Blog

www.peirenepress.com

Follow us on twitter and Facebook @PeirenePress
Peirene Press is building a community of passionate readers.
We love to hear your comments and ideas.
Please email the publisher at: meike.ziervogel@peirenepress.com

Subscribe

Peirene Press publishes series of world-class contemporary novellas. An annual subscription consists of three books chosen from across the world connected by a single theme.

The books will be sent out in December (in time for Christmas), May and September. Any title in the series already in print when you order will be posted immediately.

The perfect way for book lovers to collect all the Peirene titles.

'A class act.' GUARDIAN

'An invaluable contribution to our cultural life.'

ANDREW MOTION

£35   1 Year Subscription (3 books, free p&p)

£65   2 Year Subscription (6 books, free p&p)

£90   3 Year Subscription (9 books, free p&p)

Peirene Press, 17 Cheverton Road, London N19 3BB
T 020 7686 1941
E subscriptions@peirenepress.com

www.peirenepress.com/shop
with secure online ordering facility

Peirene's Series

FEMALE VOICE: INNER REALITIES

NO 1
Beside the Sea by Véronique Olmi
Translated from the French by Adriana Hunter
'It should be read.' GUARDIAN

NO 2
Stone in a Landslide by Maria Barbal
Translated from the Catalan by Laura McGloughlin and Paul Mitchell
'Understated power.' FINANCIAL TIMES

NO 3
Portrait of the Mother as a Young Woman
by Friedrich Christian Delius
Translated from the German by Jamie Bulloch
'A small masterpiece.' TLS

....

MALE DILEMMA: QUESTS FOR INTIMACY

NO 4
Next World Novella by Matthias Politycki
Translated from the German by Anthea Bell
'Inventive and deeply affecting.' INDEPENDENT

NO 5
Tomorrow Pamplona by Jan van Mersbergen
Translated from the Dutch by Laura Watkinson
'An impressive work.' DAILY MAIL

NO 6
Maybe This Time by Alois Hotschnig
Translated from the Austrian German by Tess Lewis
'Weird, creepy and ambiguous.' GUARDIAN

SMALL EPIC: UNRAVELLING SECRETS

NO 7
The Brothers by Asko Sahlberg
Translated from the Finnish by Emily Jeremiah and Fleur Jeremiah
'Intensely visual.' INDEPENDENT ON SUNDAY

NO 8
The Murder of Halland by Pia Juul
Translated from the Danish by Martin Aitken
'A brilliantly drawn character.' TLS

NO 9
Sea of Ink by Richard Weihe
Translated from the Swiss German by Jamie Bulloch
'Delicate and moving.' INDEPENDENT

....
TURNING POINT:
REVOLUTIONARY MOMENTS

NO 10
The Mussel Feast by Birgit Vanderbeke
Translated from the German by Jamie Bulloch
'An extraordinary book.' STANDPOINT

NO 11
Mr Darwin's Gardener by Kristina Carlson
Translated from the Finnish by Emily Jeremiah and Fleur Jeremiah
'Something miraculous.' GUARDIAN

NO 12
Chasing the King of Hearts by Hanna Krall
Translated from the Polish by Philip Boehm
'Unforgettable and unparalleled.' LANCASHIRE
EVENING POST

NEW IN 2014
COMING-OF-AGE: TOWARDS IDENTITY

NO 13

The Dead Lake by Hamid Ismailov

Translated from the Russian by Andrew Bromfield

'A rich, many-coloured tapestry.' INDEPENDENT

NO 14

The Blue Room by Hanne Ørstavik

Translated from the Norwegian by Deborah Dawkin

'One of the most important writers in Nordic contemporary literature.' MORGENBLADET

NO 15

Under the Tripoli Sky by Kamal Ben Hameda

Translated from the French by Adriana Hunter

'Straight out of a Vittorio de Sica film.' CULTURES SUD

Peirene Press is proud to support the Maya Centre.

The Maya Centre provides free psychodynamic counselling and group psychotherapy for women on low incomes in London. The counselling is offered in many different languages, including Arabic, Turkish and Portuguese. The centre also undertakes educational work on women's mental health issues.

By buying this book you help the Maya Centre to continue their pioneering services.
Peirene Press will donate 50p from the sale of this book to the Maya Centre.

www.mayacentre.org.uk